RATTLED

The Sierra Files, Book 3

By Christy Barritt

CHRISTY BARRITT

CHRISTY BARRITT

CHAPTER 1

"So, what exactly is the problem?" I pushed my glasses up higher on my nose and gently bounced my three-month-old son on my shoulder as my intern, Mandee Melkins, paused outside a tattered apartment door.

The college-aged girl pressed her thin lips together in apprehension as she fiddled with the key in the lock. Since I'd known Mandee, she'd always acted nervous and often too eager to please. She'd just started working with me a month ago at Animal Protective Services, formerly called Paws and Fur Balls, an animal rights nonprofit, and was already driving me crazy.

Mandee's request for me to meet her here today had almost pushed me over the edge. She had a tendency to be high maintenance, asking for way too much clarification on every assignment I'd given her. She often lingered, waiting for my approval—and praise—on everything she did. She worked late just so she could talk to me, which, unfortunately, was the last thing I wanted.

I'd left the office to meet Mandee after she called

me in a panic about thirty minutes ago. She wouldn't tell me what was going on, only that she desperately needed my help and it couldn't wait and no one else would do.

So here I was. With my baby. With piles of paperwork waiting for me back at the office. At a strange apartment building probably ten minutes away from my own apartment in Norfolk, Virginia.

"Thanks for coming, Sierra. I can't describe my dilemma, exactly. It's better if you see for yourself." Mandee finally managed to unlock the door before shoving it open with a dramatic push. "To start with, I guess I should tell you that this isn't my place. I've been watching my friend Patrick's apartment while he's out of town."

I stepped inside behind her, wishing we could speed all of this up. Times like this—my impatient times—made me question how good a mother I was going to be. Weren't mothers supposed to be exceedingly patient and nurturing? I wasn't sure I'd earned those titles yet, and that scared me as I thought about the future. I only wanted the best for Reef.

The inside of Patrick's apartment smelled like animals and dirty socks and microwaved meals. And Patrick was obviously a slob because trash littered every available surface and made me not want to touch anything. Mandee was a better person than me for agreeing to stay here.

The only things about the apartment that had any appeal were the huge framed photos on the walls. A close-up of a lizard's eye, mysterious and haunting. A snake's upraised head as he stared at something unknown in the distance. A frog with his tongue extended toward a fly on the rock in front of him.

"Patrick loves snakes," Mandee continued. "All reptiles and amphibians, for that matter. He thinks they're super-duper adorable." As if to confirm it, she leaned toward an aquarium in the living room, where some aquatic frogs swam, and made a baby face at them. "Because you all are."

I wanted to roll my eyes.

I'd hired Mandee after reading her uber-impressive résumé. At age fourteen, she'd not only started a citywide campaign in her hometown of Annapolis, Maryland, where she'd raised $10,000 for a local animal shelter, but she'd also collected a whole truckload of dog food, bowls, beds, and more.

She continued with her campaign until she graduated from high school, and now she was studying business with the hopes of becoming a full-time fundraiser for animal-worthy causes. The achievement was definitely something to take note of. In my postpartum rush, I'd hired her on her résumé alone.

Then I'd met her in person on her first day on the job. She looked more like a little girl than a junior in college. More often than not, she donned leggings, colorful Keds, and oversized T-shirts, usually in varying shades of pink or purple. Sometimes she wore her brown hair in braids with clips on the ends.

She had the personality to match her appearance. Despite my initial misgivings, I decided to stand by my hasty hiring decision. Someone who'd done so many good things couldn't be all that bad, right?

"So who is this Patrick guy, exactly? A friend? Family member?" I asked, still bouncing Reef on my shoulder.

"Just a friend. We were in crew together last spring, and we bonded over our love for animals."

"I understand." I'd bonded with many people over that common trait.

"Anyway, he's down in Costa Rica because he won a trip after entering a contest on the back of a cereal box or something. He's down in the rain forest, where there's no cell service. Can you imagine not having cell service—"

"Mandee," I interrupted. "Forget about the oyster and get to the pearl."

I hadn't used that expression in years. My dad used to say it all the time, and it drove me crazy.

Whatever the method or word choice, I had to get Mandee focused again. I wasn't sure how long Reef would stay quiet and happy, but I knew I was on borrowed time. At any moment now, he could start howling, wanting either food or sleep or having gas.

Little three-month-old boys weren't much different than their grown counterparts.

"Oh, right. This way." She led me down a short hallway and came to a stop in front of a room.

She seemed to hesitate a moment before pushing

the door open. When she did, I spotted a dark room filled with various terrariums. There were probably ten of them on different tables and stands along the edges of the space. The one directly beside me had a gecko inside.

I sucked in a quick breath when I saw what was inside the rest of them.

Snakes. There were snakes in these glass enclosures. All kinds of snakes, at that. I recognized a few of them but wished I didn't.

I might fight for the rights of animals across the country—the world, for that matter—but snakes still gave me the creeps.

"This happened," Mandee said.

I glanced at the tank she pointed to. It was huge—and I do mean huge. If I had to guess, it held at least sixty gallons. "That's quite a terrarium."

"It's actually a vivarium."

I scowled and pulled Reef closer to me, choosing to let her correction slide. Respect for authority from my employees was important, but my time was more valuable than a reprimand right now. I didn't want to think about what had lived in that space. I might have a degree from Yale, but sometimes emotions still trumped education.

"What happened, Mandee?"

"A thirteen-foot lavender albino ball python was in there."

"What do you mean, it *was* in there?" A shiver rushed through me, and I held Reef closer.

Mandee frowned and shook her head, still staring

at the empty tank. "Chalice was snug as a bug in her little glass house last night. I fed her, just like Patrick told me. Then I closed the door and assumed everything was as I left it. I didn't bother to check on the snakes again until after I got back from my last class. When I came in here, her enclosure was empty."

I glanced behind me this time, my thoughts filled with visions of an ugly snake eating my baby. I believed in animals being treated well . . . but I wasn't sure how I'd react if any animal ever put my baby in danger. I think I'd go all Mama Bear on the creature, and my career with APS would thus be over. Yet, it would be worth it if it meant protecting my son.

I had to stay focused here. I was the director of a national nonprofit. Respected in the field. I'd written papers and articles that had been published internationally.

This was no time to look weak or wishy-washy.

"Did you latch the lid?" I peered closer at the little hooks there.

Mandee squirmed. "They're broken. I didn't think it would be a big deal. I mean, if she got out, she'd stay in this room, right? Besides, Patrick must not have thought it was a very big deal because he didn't say anything."

Irritation rose in me, but when Reef cooed on my shoulder, the emotion dissipated. I kissed his head, mentally kicking myself for not leaving him at home. But Chad—my husband and Reef's dad—had a big construction job out in West Virginia that he was getting ready for today, and he couldn't have easily watched Reef either. I just wasn't ready to find a permanent sitter for my baby. He belonged with me. It was the way nature had intended, and no one was going to change my mind about that.

"Did you look everywhere for her?" I finally asked.

She nodded. "I looked all around the apartment. Kitchen cabinets. Under the couch. Even in my bed. She's nowhere. But it's strange because snakes like that can't just disappear. I mean, she has to be somewhere . . . unless a snake rapture happened."

I tried not to sigh. But Mandee drove me absolutely crazy with her cutesy sayings and her hunger to impress. I wanted to help her, but I was so tired, and I felt like everyone needed me. I was being pulled in too many different directions, and every route seemed important.

"You're sure she's not in the apartment?"

Mandee shrugged like she didn't have a care in the world. "It's kind of hard to hide a snake like that."

"That's true," I conceded. "But she didn't just disappear. You're right about that. You didn't hear anything last night?"

She pushed her glasses up on her nose. I noticed that she'd gotten some plastic frames a couple of weeks ago that were almost like mine. It was probably a coincidence, but it was a little strange. The only real difference in our frames was that hers were pink.

What kind of respectable adult wore pink frames?

"No, not really," she said.

"What do you mean: not really?"

She shrugged, almost looking sheepish. "A local theater was doing an all-night marathon of *My Little Pony* cartoons. I only lasted until 3:30. I know it sounds weird. I wasn't sure if I should mention it."

I had so much I could say about that, but I kept it all to myself for the sake of remaining civil. "We've got a problem here, Mandee."

"That's why I called you." Mandee beamed. "You're the smartest person I know. If anyone can locate this snake, it's you."

Being up on a pedestal had both its perks and its downfalls. This would be a downfall. Snake hunting wasn't at the top of my priority list.

I sighed and glanced around. "Was the window open?"

"Nope. Already checked. It was locked and secure. All the windows were."

"There are really so few options as to where she could have gone." I began pacing the room. Every time I passed one of the snakes, I shivered. Why anyone would want to keep one of these reptiles in their home was beyond me. They deserved to be in nature . . . far, far away from humans.

I paused by one of the terrariums. It rested on a stand against the wall, and a corn snake tried climbing up the glass inside. He wavered back and forth as if something invisible teased him.

Something on the floor behind the wooden base of

the vivarium didn't look right.

"Look at this, Mandee." I pointed to the tight, narrow space between the stand and the wall.

She squeezed beside me and squatted for a better look.

"It's an AC vent." She said it dead serious, like I'd lost my mind.

I stopped myself before scowling at her. "Exactly. But it's not on correctly."

She scooted the terrarium out of the way to get a better look. Sure enough, there was a six-inch gap where the wooden floor and the metal sides of the vent cover were supposed to meet.

"You don't think . . ." Mandee looked up at me, and her lips parted in horror.

"I think that's where the snake went," I told her bluntly.

"But that would mean . . ."

"That Chalice could be anywhere in this building." I cringed at the thought. A snake that large was nothing to be played with.

She fanned her face. "Oh, that's bad. That's really bad. I've got to find Chalice, Sierra!"

* * *

An hour later, Mandee and I had knocked on every door in the apartment complex. Five other residents checked their apartments and hadn't found anything unusual or frightening slithering through their space. I didn't think they realized just how large the snake was because everyone looked behind pillows and potted plants. I didn't bother to correct them; it was better if they didn't know what they were up against.

Only one person hadn't answered their door, and, unfortunately, it was located on the first floor right below Patrick's apartment. Sensibly speaking, this apartment was the most likely place for the snake to go while slithering through the ductwork.

"They could be at work," I said as we stood outside the door.

Mandee shrugged. "Could be."

"You know anything about whoever lives here?" Reef had fallen asleep, and right now he nestled against my chest, looking absolutely adorable. I could stare at him all day.

If only I didn't have to work or help find this snake.

Mandee shrugged again and frowned. "The guy's name is Tag. He's not very friendly. At least, that's been my impression when our paths have crossed. I really can't remember anything else about him."

"Look, like I said, he's probably at work. Why don't we walk outside and see if we can look into his apartment? If the snake's in there, maybe we'll see her. We can call the landlord and, with any luck, the snake will be gone before Tag gets home from work."

"I knew you'd know exactly what to do. Thanks, Sierra!" She threw her arms around me and nearly woke up Reef.

Honestly, I wasn't much of a hugger. Even in the post-pregnancy hormonal craziness, I still wasn't a hugger. But I knew the sentiment behind Mandee's action was respectable. And Reef didn't wake up, so it was all good.

We stepped out into the warm September day. I dodged a few generic-looking shrubs around the perimeter of the faded yellow-brick building and stretched on my tiptoes near the first window. Thankfully, the shades were open so I could see inside with relative ease. The glare of the low-hanging September sun partly obstructed my view.

I cupped my hands around my eyes and squinted, trying to get a better look. I spotted a navy-blue couch, an oversized recliner, and a kitchen beyond that.

My perusal came to an abrupt stop, though.

What was that?

I pushed myself up farther on my toes, desperate to get a better look.

It couldn't be . . .

But it was.

Two legs stuck out on the other side of the couch. And an extremely long, scary tail poked out beside it.

I'd found the snake, but, unfortunately, it appeared to be too late.

CHAPTER 2

Thirty minutes later, the police were on the scene, as well as Animal Control, an ambulance, and a fire truck. The medical examiner and her team hauled Tag from his apartment on a gurney, with a sheet over his face.

I closed my eyes as he passed, offering a moment of respect for the dead.

Death by a snake squeezing all the air out of you wasn't something I'd wish on my worst enemy. And I had a lot of evil, vile enemies—people who killed for profit. Who killed *animals* for profit, I should clarify. But, in my book, that was a wretched thing to do, especially when people did it so they could have a leather coat or a good steak dinner or a comfy down blanket.

Lives were more important than comfort or style or cravings.

As officials put Tag into the back of a van, the Animal Control folks tried to capture Chalice, the python and a cold-blooded killer. Last I'd heard, she'd slithered under a bed and officials were trying to get her out while remaining unscathed.

I'd overheard some of the officers talking about some manure on the bottom of Tag's work boots. Apparently, he'd been out on a farm for some reason. That scent of livestock would have lured a snake like Chalice right down to the apartment, and Tag would have seemed like a lamb ripe for the slaughter, especially if he was sleeping.

Could one really blame the snake for doing what she'd done? I was sure they would. But the snake was just doing what her nature led her to do. She was programmed, by instinct, to look for food and to watch out for enemies.

Mandee sobbed in the parking lot while pacing and mumbling, "This is my fault. It's all my fault."

"You couldn't have known," I told her for the twentieth time. I'd given up trying to give her any awkward pats on the back. I was still new at this motherly, nurturing type of thing. It seemed to come naturally only with Reef and no one else.

The police had already questioned Mandee and me when they first arrived on the scene. We explained everything that happened, and the detective asked us to hang around, which was getting tricky with Reef, who was on the edge of stirring.

His precious little arms stretched, and his mouth made a suckling motion, but his eyes remained closed.

I glanced at my watch, suddenly feeling anxious. Reef's sleep time was my work time. It was the only way I could manage everything—and *managing* was a strong word. I was *handling* things, at best.

I had a million things to do at home—I couldn't seem to stay on top of my to-do list now that I was a mom, and that included my schedule for both work and home. I was trying to balance both and doing a terrible job at the moment. Thankfully, Chad was gracious and didn't seem to mind that laundry piled up, dust gathered, and cat hair formed small kittens in the corners.

Tag's death was a terrible tragedy, but that was all. There was no malicious intent or premeditation. It was a horrible accident that no one could have foreseen.

Right now, a detective questioned the neighbor across the hall from Patrick. She was a forty-something woman who was considerably overweight and had bushy, brown hair. We'd talked to her right before we'd gone outside and seen the snake.

She'd told Mandee and me that she hadn't seen any snakes and that she hated snakes, for that matter, and if she did see a snake, she'd be suing Patrick—right after she cut the snake's head off. She'd react first and think later.

The neighbor seemed as animated and opinionated as I expected as the detective questioned her. Perhaps it was because she had his rapt attention and, whether he liked it or not, he had no choice but to listen as she gave her statement.

"Did your neighbor Tag have any problems with anyone?" the thirty-something detective with rumpled clothes and coffee breath asked. Detective DePalma was his name.

The woman—I thought her name was Angel—shook her head before stopping abruptly. "I would say no, in general. He was a pretty affable guy. But, now that I think about it, I did see him arguing with someone in the hallway yesterday."

Detective DePalma shifted, probably grateful for the break so his ears could have a rest. "Who was that?"

Angel's eyes scanned the parking lot before coming to a stop. She raised her arm until one finger pointed across the lot. "Her."

I followed the invisible line, knowing before I reached the end whom she was pointing at.

Mandee.

My intern let out a gasp and then, "No. No. No. No."

The word came more quickly and loudly the more she said it.

And all of that was enough to wake Reef from his slumber. He let out a wail.

And my day just got a lot longer.

***

"It wasn't like that." Mandee ran a hand through her hair again. She'd done it so many times that her bangs were getting greasy and beginning to stand up straight like a crowned crane's feathers. "I promise."

"Tell me one more time about the argument with this man the neighbors called Tag," Detective DePalma said.

I rejoined the conversation after feeding Reef. I resisted the urge to glance at my watch because I knew that would be rude. However, I had so much to do—had I mentioned that? My to-do list consumed my thoughts.

Piles of work still waited for me from my maternity leave. I hadn't even gotten a shower this morning because, once I'd finally gotten to sleep, I'd overslept.

I didn't like my life being out of order, and having a baby seemed like the perfect formula for things getting crazy. But as I glanced down at a sleepy Reef, I smiled.

I knew I wouldn't trade him for anything. Ever. He and Chad were the best things to happen to me.

"It was no big deal. I'm just here pet-sitting—"

Animal-companion sitting, I mentally corrected her. First rule of being an animal rights activist: realizing that people don't have pets. People had companion animals because that showed we were all sharing this thing called life together.

"When did you start pet-sitting?" Detective DePalma asked.

"Two days ago on Tuesday." Just as Mandee finished her sentence, a team of men from Animal Control emerged from the apartment building holding Chalice.

The snake was huge—and I do mean huge. Mandee had said thirteen feet, but I calculated her to be longer. And if it took five men to carry her out, she must be heavy.

She had lovely yellow spots, though, and subtle lavender-tinted skin beneath. Even with the pretty coloring, I still shuddered as they passed us. I wouldn't want to tangle with that snake. No way. Nor would I want a snake like that living anywhere near my apartment building.

"Where's the tenant of the apartment . . ." He looked down at a pad of paper in his hands. "Mr. Patrick Roper?"

"He's in the rain forest of Costa Rica until late next week. He knew he wouldn't have cell service, so he didn't even take his phone. He's a free spirit like that." Mandee tugged at her braid.

"How many snakes does he have?" The detective sounded monotone and really quite uninterested in all of this. And his coffee breath could be smelled from two feet away. That had to be some kind of record.

How could he be uninterested? I was sure this would be the talk of the precinct. Those cops were used to shootings and drug overdoses and domestic violence. All those things were terrible. *Terrible.*

But death by a snake? This was the stuff water-cooler conversations thrived on.

"Seven," Mandee said. "There were seven snakes. One gecko. Two frogs."

The detective slid his sunglasses on as the sun sank lower behind us—in front of him—and created a blinding glare. "And are you a snake specialist?"

Mandee blinked, three clumps of hair still standing

up straight and making her look a little crazy. But it was her wide eyes that stopped me in my tracks. They were so circular that, for a minute, she reminded me of a . . . snake.

"A snake specialist?" She asked the question it as if she might be contemplating affirming the statement. "No, I just like animals. I wanted to help my friend out."

"When was the last time you saw . . ." He glanced at his pad of paper. "Chalice?"

She rubbed her hands on her jeans and swallowed hard. "Last night when I fed her. She looked perfectly content. Everything looked normal, and, I assure you, there were no red flags."

"Uh huh." The detective didn't look or sound impressed. "And did you put the lid back on the snake's habitat?"

"Of course, I did!" Her face dropped. "I think. I mean, I usually do. What if I didn't? But the latch was broken. I figured it was okay, though."

I closed my eyes. The poor girl was just digging her hole deeper and deeper. I wanted to intercede, but I wasn't sure how to help. I had a tendency to stir up trouble instead of settle it down, despite what I considered good intentions.

The detective shifted and raised his chin. I couldn't see his eyes because of his sunglasses, but I'd bet they were full of doubt.

"So it's a possibility that the lid wasn't all the way on?" he asked.

Mandee shrugged, the whites of her eyes visible again. "I suppose."

"Is it also a possibility that you moved the vent cover out of the way in hopes that the snake might make a visit to Tag?" There was no humor in the detective's voice. No humor at all—only accusation.

Mandee gasped again. "No! I had no idea that vent cover wasn't all the way on. Why would I? I didn't make it a habit to check behind all the tables in the room. I just assumed things were in place and as they should be. You can ask Sierra. She was the one who found the vent."

Detective DePalma turned toward me, and I forced a smile and a wave. Here I was, trying to stay out of things and be a good mom while still maintaining my job and life's passion. How had I gotten drawn into all of this?

At that moment, my cell phone rang in my back pocket. It was probably Chad calling to check on Reef. The man was obsessed with his baby. He called whenever he had the chance and even liked to talk *ga ga goo goo* into the phone.

I thought it was adorable.

I ignored the beeping sound and kept my attention on the detective. "It's true. I did notice the vent wasn't fully on. I realized the snake had to go somewhere, that she hadn't disappeared into thin air. With all of the windows closed and no sign of her in the apartment, I figured she'd gotten out some other way."

"I see." The detective bobbed his head up and down like a fishing lure on a balmy day.

But all the pieces had fallen in place too easily, hadn't they? The latch was broken. The vent cover moved. The neighbor had smelled like farm animals, which had probably lured Chalice right to him.

I didn't believe in coincidences of those proportions.

"But there's one other thing you haven't considered," I continued, kicking myself for getting involved. But I just couldn't stop myself.

"What's that?"

I launched my theory out there, knowing good and well it might sound crazy. "What if someone took the snake and moved the vent cover to make it appear she'd escaped? Maybe this isn't Mandee's fault at all."

The detective blinked at me like I was a moron. It was times like these I wanted to pull out my college degree, all of my awards and accolades, and display them proudly. But I couldn't fall back on those things. I could only stand on my strengths of the moment.

The fact that I had spit-up on my shoulder probably didn't do much for my credibility.

"Why would someone do that?" the detective asked.

"Maybe they wanted the snake for themselves. Or maybe they didn't like it in the apartment building and wanted to get rid of it," I offered.

Detective DePalma actually pulled his sunglasses down and stared me in the eye for a moment. "So how would it have ended up in Mr. Wilson's apartment then?"

I shrugged. "Who knows? We don't know who has a key to Patrick's apartment, who knew the snakes were there, or who knew Patrick was out of town. Maybe Tag Wilson took the snake himself but quickly discovered she was too much to handle."

I thought my theory sounded plausible. My best friend, Gabby, who had a habit of getting involved in police investigations, would be proud right now. I was thinking like she did.

The detective scooted his glasses back up and turned toward Mandee, totally dismissing my theory. "Tell me about your argument with Tag."

Mandee frowned again. "Argument is such a strong word. We simply had a disagreement. I like to do Zumba every morning at 6 a.m. That's not a problem in my own apartment because I live on the first floor. Well, apparently, I was waking up Tag every morning because the walls of this place—and the ceilings—are super thin or something. He was very angry with me."

"Did you come to a compromise?"

Mandee shook her head. "It's a free country. If I don't do Zumba in the morning, then I have no other time to do it. And if I don't exercise, I get very cranky. And if I get cranky, I'm not fun to live with or be near. He was just going to have to get over it. Besides, I was only going to be here for a week. He could live with it."

I closed my eyes again. The poor girl wasn't doing herself any favors. Every time she opened her mouth, the whole situation seemed to get worse and worse. I knew what that was like. I didn't generally care when I ruffled feathers. But watching someone else dig her own grave made me want to intercede for her.

"I suppose he didn't react well to that?" The detective eyed Mandee like a one-hundred-dollar prize at a turkey shoot. He was seeing a trophy on his badge, another case he could solve and get accolades for. And poor Mandee was offering no resistance.

"He didn't. He went ballistic. Said something about his job going south, bills piling up, and life stinking. Then he said things were going to turn around. That he had a plan."

"A plan?"

She shrugged. "No idea."

"Even after hearing that, you still didn't change your mind or your routine? Your morning exercise remained the same?" the detective asked.

"Well, I felt sorry for him. Of course. But life is hard. People who think the world is all about them really get on my nerves. They need to learn that other people have rights also." She glanced at me. "Other animals too, for that matter."

She was on the verge of being arrested and still trying to impress me? I didn't know if I should be annoyed or flattered.

Detective DePalma sighed. "Did he make you mad enough that you turned Chalice lose, hoping the snake might teach Tag a lesson? Maybe you didn't intend to kill him. Just scare him."

Mandee's eyes widened again. "I would never."

I put my hand on her arm. I had to stop this. Now. "Before you say anything else, I suggest you get a lawyer, Mandee."

"But—"

I raised my hand to stop her. "Really. This is one rabbit hole—or should I say snake hole—you don't want to go down."

CHAPTER 3

I finally got back to my apartment just after the sun fully set, but Chad wasn't there. I frowned. I'd looked forward to running my day past him and hearing his insight into all the craziness that had ensued. That would have to wait until he returned home.

I already had a headache forming, I had no idea what to fix for dinner, and Reef was wide awake, while all I wanted to do was sleep. This was life as a working mom, and I was still adjusting.

I placed Reef in a little bouncy seat that he seemed to love and then stood in the middle of my living room, unable to move or think. Our two-bedroom apartment was home sweet home for me, but it was beginning to feel cramped. At any given time, I had at least three cats because I often took in strays until I could find them another home. Now that Reef was here and baby stuff had invaded any free space, my abode felt cramped. Chad and I were saving money so we could upgrade, but we still had a ways to go.

At the moment, the place smelled like patchouli. Whenever I finally made myself move, I'd turn on my *Sounds of Nature* CD. I especially found the whales and "Song of the Seashore" tracks calming.

Before I could do anything, a knock sounded at my door and someone pushed her way inside. Apparently, I hadn't locked the door behind me.

"Hey, Sierra. I thought I heard you come in."

It was my best friend, Gabby, who also happened to live upstairs. She was wearing her signature outfit: jeans, flip-flops, and a snarky T-shirt, which read "I don't want to adult today."

She looked especially perky at the moment. Even her curly hair looked cheerful. Honestly, she'd looked happy in the past few months. Really happy. It might have something to do with her current relationship status: taken and serious.

She immediately went to Reef and rubbed her finger against his tiny hand. "How's my favorite little boy today?" she cooed.

People had a tendency to ignore me when Reef was around, but I was okay with that. I would ignore me if Reef was around, so I understood.

"Can you hold him a minute?" I asked.

"You betcha." She eased him from the bouncy seat and cradled him against her. Her entire body seemed to go soft and gooey as soon as she touched him. "He's so precious. Have I told you that yet?"

"Every time you see him."

"Well, he's one loved little boy." Gabby swayed back and forth like a natural.

I'd never seen my best friend like this before. I wasn't sure how I expected her to act once the baby came, but she'd always been the independent and tough type. I'd never seen her play with kids or even really talk to them before. Reef had flipped some kind of internal switch, and she was going to win the godmother of the year award.

"How was your day?" Gabby dragged her gaze away from Reef, seeming to sense something was wrong.

I sighed and plopped down in a rocking chair I'd tucked away in the corner. "It was long. I think we've switched lives. My day seemed much more appropriate for a Day-in-the-Life-of-Gabby St. Claire than a day in my life."

"Oh . . . please, do tell. What happened?" She sat down on the couch, still snuggling Reef in her arms.

I could see his hands reaching for her red hair and the start of a smile on his lips. He cooed and seemed just as in love with her as she seemed with him.

I waited until Gabby glanced at me. I needed evidence that Reef's spell on her wasn't all-consuming before I wasted my breath. As the saying went, this wasn't my first rodeo. And rodeos were horrible events, just in case you wondered about my stance on them.

"You have my full attention. I promise." Gabby looked both curious and slightly apologetic when she realized I was waiting for her.

I gave her the rundown on today's events. Her eyes widened with each new fact. They didn't widen so much with shock or horror. They widened with hunger.

Gabby *loved* stuff like this. Not the death part, but the figuring out things part. She'd started as a crime-scene cleaner, but worked for a forensic technology company now. It was the next best thing for her to being an actual forensic detective. She had a knack for investigations and was somewhat of a local legend after she'd solved a few cases that had stumped law enforcement.

"A room full of snakes?" Gabby shook her head, her curls bouncing around her face with the action. "Did you feel *hiss*-terical?"

I would have thrown something at her if I had the energy. "You're so funny."

She smiled mischievously. "Yeah, I think so."

She looked off into the distance and, in her most melodramatic expression, began singing a song I'd never heard

I only stared at her. She was known for bursting spontaneously into song, so this wasn't unusual.

She stopped after a few minutes and shrugged. "'Union of the Snake'?"

I shook my head.

"Duran Duran?"

"I've heard of them."

"It's a strange song with an even stranger music video. I know you have tons of free time—" She cleared her throat and smiled mischievously. "You'll have to check it out sometime."

I looked more closely at Reef, noticing his hands

were no longer reaching for her hair. "Did you get him to sleep?"

She glanced at Reef and shrugged. "It appears so. That was fast."

How had she done that? And while singing that awful song, at that. "He screamed the entire way home. I begged him just to go to sleep. Now look at you. You've got the touch."

She smiled and looked down at him again. Her smile disappeared as she looked back up at me. "As much as I would love to talk about all of my finest attributes for the rest of the evening, let's talk about the snake instead. So, do the police think it was manslaughter? Was your friend charged?"

"I told Mandee to get a lawyer and that she shouldn't say anything else until she did. Then Reef had a blowout, and I really had no choice at that point but to leave. You would know better than I would, but I doubt the cops have enough evidence to arrest her. But she kept digging herself into a hole and incriminating herself with every word she spoke."

"She could be charged with involuntary manslaughter, if nothing else. The fight she had with her neighbor doesn't do much for her case, either. Still, I doubt arguing about Zumba is a strong enough motive for murder."

"Well, I'll call her in the morning and see what's going on. Right now, I've got to tend to my own flock. Starting with dinner. I have no idea what to make."

RATTLED

I ran through the possibilities. Tofu stir-fry? Chad hated stir-fry. Lentil tacos? I was nearly certain I was out of my stockpile of that particular legume. A nice, big salad? Chad was usually famished by the time he finished working, so I had a feeling a salad wouldn't cut it.

Cooking for both of us had proven to be a challenge.

"I have some vegetable soup upstairs. Would you like some? Riley's working late, so it's just me."

My spirits lifted for a moment. "Did you use chicken broth?"

She shook her head. "Nope. Not because I didn't want to but because I didn't have any. I'm pretty sure it's a totally vegan soup. Beans, corn, peppers, onions, tomatoes, and herbs."

I felt so grateful that I almost cried. I knew it was an overreaction, but all my emotions felt bigger than necessary lately. "I'd *love* some. It would be one less thing for me to think about tonight."

Gabby nodded and smiled. "I'll bring it down in a minute for you. I just need a little more Reef time."

I really couldn't ask for a better best friend. I had a tendency to be a little bristly, yet Gabby still loved me, despite me.

After our conversation, life suddenly didn't feel quite as overwhelming.

That's what friends were for.

***

33

That night, I got a phone call from Mandee at 3:30 a.m. Yes, 3:30. After. Midnight.

Apparently, the police didn't believe in letting people sleep and *then* arresting them. No, when they decided to arrest someone, they arrested someone right then.

And that person was Mandee.

What person was I? I was the kind who wore the title: No Rest for the Weary.

"There were pry marks found on the vent, Sierra," Mandee rushed, her voice close to hysterical. "The police think I intentionally did this."

Concern clutched my muscles at her announcement. "They could arrest you on that? Isn't it circumstantial?"

"Well . . ." Agitation crept into her voice. "They also found a crowbar with my fingerprints on it."

I sat up straight in bed, trying not to wake Chad but unable to actually move to a different room. My body wasn't cooperating. "What? Where?"

She sniffled. "In the dumpster behind the apartment building."

I shook my head, unable to fathom how all of this had played out, still trying to get the cobwebs out of my head. "How did that happen?"

"It's a long story. But it's not because I pried the vent off."

I let out a sigh, trying to collect my thoughts and not fall back asleep in the process. Everything I'd just learned made it appear that Mandee had motive, means, and opportunity. I didn't have to be a detective to figure that out.

"I don't know what to say, Mandee." At least, I didn't know what to say that would make her feel better. I was leaning toward trying to prep her for a prison stay.

"Sierra, I can only talk on the phone for a few more minutes. Can you come to the police station? Please."

In an instant, I collected my thoughts both quickly and efficiently. Somehow I had moved from her boss to her confidante, and now I was supposed to be her savior. The problem was that I'd only agreed to be her boss.

"They probably won't let me see you," I finally said, the dark room and my comfy bed mocking me. Mandee probably wished that was her biggest worry, which made me feel a rush of guilt.

"I can't afford a lawyer. My parents are at some spa in Iceland. I need your help. I'm not going to get a fair shot here, Sierra."

I ran a hand over my face, trying to formulate what to say. Before I could, Mandee continued.

"There's one other thing," Mandee continued.

I braced myself for whatever that was. Could this really get worse? "What's that?"

"You know that conversation I said I had with Tag earlier in the week? The argument, I should say. Well, I ended it by saying something like, 'I hope one of those snakes thinks of you as dinner and squeezes the living daylights out of you.'"

Before I could stop myself, a moan escaped.

"I know," she cried. "It sounds bad, doesn't it? Please, can you try to come down here?"

"I'm not a lawyer."

"But you're the smartest person I know."

"That doesn't mean they'll let me talk to you."

"Could you at least try?

I threw my legs over the side of the bed, knowing I'd crossed over to her side. There was no way I was getting out of helping her right now. The girl had no one else.

"I'll see what I can do," I finally said. "But I can't promise anything."

She let out a half-moan, half-sigh. "I knew you'd look out for me, Sierra. You're like the big sister I never had."

The big sister she never had? Something stirred inside me. She'd gotten to me. Maybe that had been the entire point. But now I knew it would be hard to say no.

I hung up and stood, pulling on some jeans and my favorite navy-blue shirt. I wouldn't look like much when I got down to the police station, but at least I'd be there.

"Can't she get out on bail?" Chad said, still looking sleepy.

I shook my head. "No bail. Not yet, at least. What's on your schedule today?"

"I've got to finish that house with the water damage and then get ready for the job in West Virginia."

"The one for your friend? The old theme park?"

He nodded. "That's the one. Mythical Falls. I leave this weekend. You didn't forget, did you?"

Had I forgotten? I couldn't remember anything lately. "No, of course I didn't forget."

He was leaving *this* weekend. Wow. How would I ever get everything done without him here? I couldn't think about it now.

"Why are you asking about my schedule today?" Chad ran a hand through his hair, but it looked no different than usual. He always had the bedhead look.

"Mandee asked me to come down to the police station. She's scared, and she doesn't have any family here. I have the impression she doesn't have any friends here either."

"Sounds like a hard place to be." He drew in a long, deep breath before nodding. "I can keep Reef until ten, but then I really have to get to work. Maybe Clarice could come by and babysit?"

I slipped on some loafers. "Maybe. I'm hoping I won't be gone that long. I want to help Mandee, but I don't know what I can do. She needs to talk to a lawyer. Even Gabby. But this isn't my specialty."

Just as I grabbed my purse, I heard a cry from the other room. Reef.

Chad moaned.

"I'm sorry," I told him.

My heart longed to go get my son and have some time with him. But I didn't want to take him to the police station with me. Some places just weren't meant for babies.

"Yeah, me too." He threw the covers off. "I guess I'll get an early start to my day."

CHAPTER 4

By the time I got to the police station, I was grumpier than I'd been after initially being woken up. My crankiness had increased with every rotation of my tires. I was irritated at Mandee, at Chalice, and even at the police. Certainly the cops couldn't hold Mandee on this circumstantial evidence, and that's exactly what I told them.

"Circumstantial or not, she's being charged," Detective DePalma told me with an annoyed sigh. He stared at me from across the busy hallway where officers and those they arrested were shuffled from Point A to Point B.

I crossed my arms, wishing I knew as much about the justice system as I did about animal rights. "Fingerprints on a crowbar are hardly evidence at all."

I wasn't sure that was totally true, but Mandee was not the type to have killer instincts. She was the type who loved puppy dogs and unicorns and cotton candy.

The detective's nostrils twitched. "Those fingerprints prove that she handled the tool. She must have used it to pry the vent cover away from the floor, which then allowed the snake to get out and go through the ductwork into her neighbor's apartment. Flecks of metal from the vent cover were found on the crowbar and visa versa. She's looking at involuntary manslaughter. No one really thinks she wanted to kill her downstairs neighbor—probably just scare him."

I threw my hands in the air. "You're talking in probabilities! You can't build a case on that."

He leveled his gaze at me, appearing especially tired, as the bags under his eyes looked puffy and wrinkled. Earlier, his sunglasses had masked both of those things well. "We can and we will."

"What about the snake's owner? Patrick?"

"We're trying to reach him, but he's apparently out of the country." He scowled again. "Now, would you like a few minutes with Ms. Melkins or not?"

I scowled, trying to rack my brain for anything else that I should be asking or pleading for. I came up blank, which was highly unusual for me.

"Yes, I would like a few minutes with Mandee." I couldn't believe I was actually getting to see her. I figured she'd be in a cell right now and able to talk only to a lawyer.

He led me down another hallway and into a room with a large table and three chairs. There was a strange scent in the room—a mix of body odor and Lysol. The combination wasn't pleasant. Everything in the room was gray, and I wondered if this was the police department's effort to play mind games and make those they arrested feel even bleaker in hopes they'd simply confess.

I didn't feel comfortable enough to sit—not when I had so much on my mind—so, instead, I paced. I hated feeling clueless. No, I was Mrs. Informed and Prepared, the woman who read every book I could on subjects so I could be well-educated. I had a whole shelf of books on parenting that I'd read in the months before Reef was born. Unfortunately, I hadn't had time to read any criminal-law manuals since Mandee had called me at 3:30 a.m.

Five minutes after I was escorted into the room, the door opened again and Mandee was led inside.

She threw her arms around me and sobbed against my shoulder. "Sierra! I'm so glad you came. I knew you wouldn't let me down."

Again, this was one of those times when I wasn't really sure I should be up on a pedestal. There was really so little I could do for Mandee, yet she thought I could walk on water. I didn't want to disappoint her, but I didn't know how *not* to in this situation. I was educated enough to know that I was setting myself up for failure, plain and simple.

"Have you hired a lawyer yet, Mandee?" I asked once she pulled away from her dramatic hug long enough to make eye contact. There was no need of getting her hopes up only to have them fall fast and hard. Violently, for that matter.

I had to admit that I missed the old Mandee.

Mandee wearing a gray jumpsuit with no colorful clips in her hair did not seem like Mandee.

We sat at the table in the center of the room so we could talk. Besides, I needed to put some distance between her and myself.

"I can't afford one." She sniffled and stared at me with puppy-dog eyes.

"The city will hire someone to represent you," I said. "It's a basic right."

"Yeah, but I don't want a court-appointed attorney. I want someone who believes me. I want you."

She was a hardhead. That was all there was to it. "But I'm not a lawyer."

She blinked back tears. "I have faith in you, Sierra. You do a good job whatever you do. It's your nature."

I sighed. She wasn't going to let this go, was she? Finally, I nodded. "Let me talk to someone for you. If I can't represent you, then he would be the next best thing. I trust him. In the meantime, is there anything you want to tell me?"

"I didn't do it."

I was going to have to approach this slowly and carefully. "How did your prints get on that crowbar? And how did it end up in the trash?"

"Easy. Patrick's dishwasher broke. I was trying to help him by putting some of his dirty dishes in it and washing them. But then smoke started coming out, and I couldn't get the dishwasher open. I was afraid the whole place would burn down."

"So you took a crowbar to his dishwasher?" Did the girl have any common sense at all?

She shrugged, looking awfully sheepish. "Well, yeah. But then I felt bad about it when I noticed the pry marks. I decided the next day, after sleeping on it, that I should get rid of the evidence."

"He'd still see the pry marks, even without the crowbar," I countered, trying to wrap my mind around her logic. How could she be so smart yet so dense?

She shrugged again and averted her gaze from mine. "I didn't think it through. At all. I may have even considered lying and saying someone broke into the apartment and did it."

"Why would someone break in and pry open a dishwasher?" How had I ever hired this woman?

"Like I said, I didn't think it all through."

"That's quite obvious." I straightened after I said the words, realizing I'd probably offended her. But, as she looked at me with those big puppy-dog eyes, I realized I hadn't. The insult had either gone right over her head or she'd ignored it.

I drew in a deep breath, trying to gather my patience. "Is there any other possible evidence the police can use against you, Mandee? Think about it."

She shook her head, moisture rimming her eyes again. The girl was scared, and that made my heart squeeze with compassion. I hated to think about Reef being left on his own to sort out something like this one day when he was older. I'd want someone to be there for him. Motherhood was changing me.

"No," Mandee said. "There's nothing I've left out. Nothing at all. I promise."

I nodded, making up my mind to help. "Okay, I'm going to see what I can do to find some answers. But I can't make any promises."

Hope lit her eyes. Not just hope. Abundant hope. Little-girl, I-still-believe-in-Santa-Claus hope. "You're the best, Sierra. The absolute best."

I stood. "I don't know about that."

"Oh, by the way, I told the detective you were a lawyer."

My eyes widened. "Why would you do that?"

"Because I thought you would represent me."

That was the reason the detective had let me back here. I knew something didn't seem right. "Mandee, it's a crime to pretend to be a lawyer. I could be arrested!"

She gave me her big, childlike eyes again. "I'm sorry. I had no idea."

"I've got to go clear this up."

"Tell them it's all my fault. The lawyer part, that is. Not the death of Tag Wilson."

I turned to leave when she called me back. I paused by the door, my muscles tightening in anticipation of what she might say this time. "Yes?"

"Would you mind feeding Patrick's geckos for me while I'm here?"

***

After I left Mandee at the jail, I decided to use my time as wisely as possibly. I went into the office—all was quiet, as no one else wanted to be there at 5:30 a.m. I would treasure the peace for a few minutes while I could.

My little office was located in a corner of a single-story building. When the sun was actually out, I could look out my windows and see a lovely view of the parking lot and the thin stretch of woods behind the building—not to mention one corner of the dumpster.

It wasn't much, but it was much better than the cubicle I'd started out in.

I spent my first hour catching up on emails and some paperwork for various campaigns we had going on. The hardest part about being director was that I couldn't be as hands-on. I ended up managing money and people more than getting directly involved in our crusades. But I'd worked hard, and it only made sense that I'd want to move up in the organization. The added responsibility had meant a pay raise, which was nice.

On a whim, in between returning emails, I decided to do a little research on Patrick. People made it way too easy to find out information on themselves by oversharing on social media. Social media worked to our favor here at APS because we used it to start campaigns, which then went viral. Most people posted too much information, though.

Like Patrick.

I went to his Facebook page, which was surprisingly public. Perhaps it was because he used it as a venue to display his photographs.

I studied his profile picture a moment. The man appeared to be on the shorter side, and he had a slight build. His hair was light brown with an almost red tint to it, and, even though he was still young, he was already getting a receding hairline.

I checked the rest of his stats. He didn't list a job, but he did list being a college student. He'd posted many, many pictures of himself with Chalice.

No pictures from the rain forest, though. Maybe that was because, as Mandee had said, he had no cell service.

As I leaned back in my chair and chewed on that thought, one of my star employees—her name was Chloe—stuck her head into my office. Personality-wise, Chloe was pretty much a mini-me. She was smart, driven, and tenacious. She loved animals with every fiber of her being and fought with every last breath to help them.

Physically speaking, she was Irish with the reddest hair I'd ever seen, pale skin, and freckles. Whereas I was short and petite, she was tall and big-boned.

Unlike Mandee, hiring Chloe had been one of my best decisions ever.

"Did you hear about the snake?" Chloe asked as she stepped into my office.

I needed to rethink my open-door policy. "Yes, I did. How did you hear?"

A wrinkle formed between her eyebrows. "Same way as everyone else. It was in the newspaper this morning."

The newspaper. Of course! Had Mandee's name been mentioned? I'd wait and see if Chloe brought it up.

"What about it?" I asked.

"Well, the snake obviously. Animal Control will most likely euthanize it."

I blinked as I processed her words. Animals were usually the first thing I thought about. But, in this case, there were too many other details, and I hadn't even thought about Chalice's fate.

"If the animal is deemed aggressive, the city usually does try to euthanize. You're right. What are you thinking?"

She slapped a paper on my desk. "I was up all night drafting this campaign after I saw the story on the evening news. What do you think?"

I picked up the first sheet and scanned it. "Animal Lives Matter?"

She nodded, fire lighting her eyes. "Brilliant, isn't it?"

"It's very . . . relevant."

"These people can't blame animals for doing what animals are programmed to do. That snake didn't know she was committing a crime. She was probably either hungry or defending herself. She doesn't deserve to die."

But she did kill someone.

The thought startled me because it was so out of the realm of the ordinary for me. Usually in cases like these I didn't see the human victims. I didn't see the way lives were turned upside down.

I only thought about the animal.

I'd seen this particular animal. She was huge. If one of my neighbors wanted to keep Chalice in their apartment, I'd feel highly uncomfortable.

"Sierra?" Chloe questioned, staring at me.

I snapped back to the present. "Yes?"

"So, what do you think?"

My team here expected me to lead them in these crusades. We tried to cause as big a ruckus as possible, knowing that it took a big ruckus to even get small results. Small ruckuses did virtually nothing.

I glanced at the paper again, quickly scanning. It included our basic press release, a virtual campaign to raise awareness, and letters to city leaders. I nodded. "Go for it."

A smile lit her face. "Great. I'll get busy."

After she scurried away, I looked up the newspaper article on my computer and gleaned the main pieces of information.

Tag Wilson was 38 years old and originally from Seattle, Washington.

Neighbors said he kept to himself.

The scent of livestock on him may have drawn the snake to him, making Chalice think he was food.

A suspect is being held in connection with the event.

Tag's picture stared at me from the front page. He had a pointy nose, heavy jowls, and thinning hair. He appeared to have a larger build but a really great, wide smile.

The timing seemed awful for a campaign like this. I was all in favor of saving the lives of animals that were mistreated. This case seemed like a gray area.

My thoughts turned to Mandee. If my research was correct, she'd have a hearing in order for bond to be set. The girl couldn't represent herself. She just couldn't.

On a whim, I called my neighbor Riley. He was an attorney. Maybe he could help.

Unfortunately, the call went straight to voice mail.

I sighed and leaned back. Before my frustration could build, my phone rang. It was Mandee calling collect, and she was crying again.

"Oh, Sierra. You'll never believe this," she started.

I leaned back in my chair and took a deep breath in. And let it out. "What's that?"

"The police are messing up everything. Everything!"

My spine stiffened at her announcement. "What do you mean?"

She hesitated before saying, "I may have put something on Facebook two nights ago that was slightly incriminating, and they're totally taking it the wrong way. They really think I intended to kill Tag."

I closed my eyes, fighting annoyance and irritation. Mandee grated on my last nerve and tested my kindness like no one else. "You mean there is more evidence out there that you didn't mention."

"I promise, I forgot all about it." Her voice sounded pleading and innocent again, like she didn't have a fault in any of this.

"What did you say on Facebook?" I braced myself for her response. There was no telling what she'd written.

"Only that I wanted to kill Tag Wilson." Her voice tapered with a touch of shame. "Strangle him. Or maybe I'd let my friend's snake do it for me."

I lowered my head until it connected with my hand in a face palm. I'd seen a lot. I'd heard a lot. And Mandee could win a prize for putting her foot in her mouth. It was almost like she *wanted* to look guilty. "Why in the world would you say that, Mandee?"

"Well, of course, I didn't mean it! He just made me so mad with his hoity-toity attitude against me doing Zumba. And then he started insulting Patrick and talking about those 'crazy animal rights activists.' He pushed me over the edge!"

"Don't tell the police that," I urged. "It can be interpreted wrong. Very wrong."

"Oh . . . of course. I would never repeat that to anyone but you. But I didn't do it, Sierra. I didn't kill him. It was just an expression."

Like the police hadn't heard *that* before. "I understand. But things keep continually coming out that you haven't told me about. It makes me feel like you're not being transparent and honest with me."

"I *am* being transparent! I'm so sorry, Sierra. I just didn't think anything about those things. Nothing at all."

I rolled my eyes, unable to take her seriously at this point. Her comprehension of the cause and effect of her actions only affirmed that she was still a child at heart.

"I understand," I finally said.

"I knew you would, Sierra. Thanks so much. Oh, and by the way: Did you feed the geckos yet?"

I rolled my eyes up toward the ceiling, praying I wouldn't break under the pressure I felt at the moment. Or strangle Mandee the next time I saw her.

"Not yet. But I'm on my way now."

CHAPTER 5

With everything crazy going on, I decided to let the landlord, who lived next door, know who I was. Then I grabbed a spare key that had been hidden beneath the doormat outside Patrick's door. Mandee had told me he kept it there.

In the back of my mind, I also realized that anyone could have gotten inside and jimmied the vent cover. The key's hiding spot wasn't remarkable, and anyone with a little bit of initiative could have found it. I stored that information away in case it became relevant later.

I slipped inside and paused. Despite the fact that I knew Chalice had been captured, that didn't stop me from surveying the space for wayward snakes. I didn't see any. Thank goodness.

Something about the place seemed eerie, but I couldn't put my finger on what. I suppose it could be how quiet it was, especially after considering all the harm one of the snakes who'd lived here had done. The snake's actions had turned one family upside down.

Though Tag didn't appear to be married or have children, certainly there was someone out there who was missing him.

Had the police contacted Patrick yet? Was he on his way home? Would someone file a civil lawsuit against him?

Pushing away my heebie-jeebies, I went into the "snake room." I quickly located a bucket full of live crickets and frowned.

"I hope you appreciate this," I muttered. I wasn't sure if I was talking to geckos, to Mandee, or to Patrick. Maybe all three.

I closed my eyes as I stuck my hand into the bucket. I managed to grab one of the crickets. I moved with lightning-fast speed as I dropped the insect into the terrarium. A shiver ran through me.

Thankfully, the snakes had to be fed only every week or so. Since they normally ate mice or other animals, I was glad I didn't have to feed them. I fought for animals not to be considered food, yet here I was, in the position to feed animals to animals next week if this fiasco wasn't resolved first.

Talk about a moral crisis.

I waited until the gecko ate the cricket before repeating the process with the frogs.

Finally, I could leave! I felt slightly guilty not giving them more attention. After all, they were here all alone now with no one to care for them. But I had bigger fish to fry.

I gasped as the thought entered my mind, almost as if God himself had heard me and was calling me out on my mental hypocrisy.

"I didn't mean it," I muttered.

It was time for me to get out of here. Now.

Before I could leave, I paused. I almost felt like something was stopping me, begging for my attention. But what?

I glanced around the kitchen. Like the rest of the house, it was messy—with dishes in the sink and pots and pans piled up on the counter.

I opened the fridge. All that was in there were orange juice and some lunchmeat. Nothing outstanding.

Out of curiosity, I opened a cabinet. I spotted several boxes of mac and cheese, some soup cans, and other easy meals, typical for a bachelor.

I paused. There was one thing I didn't see.

Cereal.

Hadn't Mandee said Patrick had won that trip because of a contest on the back of a cereal box? Yet, there was no milk in the fridge or any cereal boxes in the cabinets. I checked the rest of them, just to be sure, and confirmed my theory.

It was probably nothing—right?

But I couldn't help but think it was something.

***

As I was leaving the apartment building, the neighbor who

lived across the hall from Tag stepped out of his door and into my path. I didn't recognize him from when Mandee and I had questioned all the residents here on the day the snake went missing. No, an older woman had answered the door to this apartment.

He wore a stained wife beater T-shirt with baggy sweatpants. His hair was dark and curly and formed an almost cone-like style on the sides, reminding me of the topography of the US—mountains near the coast, plains in the middle. BO emanated from him—I could smell it even from where I stood.

"Did you just come from Patrick's apartment?" His eyes narrowed suspiciously before he raised the beer in his hand and took a long swig. "I thought I saw you go in earlier."

Who started drinking before noon? Someone with problems, that was who.

I glanced up. Based on the way the building was laid out, he would have a bird's eye view of Patrick's apartment door from here. The second and third floors were surrounded by balconies and narrow walkways, only broken up by the sweeping staircase between them.

I nodded, resisting the urge to glance at my watch. I had so much to do at work. And I hoped I'd have a moment to swing by the apartment and check on Chad and Reef. And maybe take a shower. And find something other than the week-old apple I'd found on my desk and consumed for breakfast.

For a moment, and just a moment, I imagined what

it would be like to pare down my responsibilities. To focus only on Reef for a while. To put my job on hold.

I sighed. I couldn't do that. Not only did I love my job, but Chad and I had bills to pay. Plus, I'd always been so career-oriented. Could I really ever consider giving that up? The decision seemed complex, without an easy answer.

The man at the door waited for my answer.

I snapped back to reality for long enough to state the obvious. "I did just come from Patrick's apartment. Yes."

He continued to eyeball me like I was a lion plotting to overthrow leadership of his pride. "Are you friends with *Patrick*?" He said his name like it was a bad word.

"I am not." If he thought I was going to offer more information than necessary, he was wrong. I didn't mind awkward silence. *Bring it.*

He continued to stare as if I might be a killer. "Are you with the police?"

"No." I didn't offer any more information.

After several seconds of silence, he finally said, "I heard one of his snakes killed Tag."

I nodded slowly, careful not to show any emotion that could be misinterpreted. As Mandee's friend, I had to be aware of each of my actions and every word I said. "That is true."

He shifted, his lips wrinkled as he observed me. "You know how that happened?"

"The police are looking into it."

"I heard there was malicious intent involved."

I sucked in a long breath and attempted to gather my patience. "As far as I know, no one would want to kill your neighbor. It was just a terrible accident."

He shrugged, still looking partly unconvinced and partly suspicious. "Maybe."

You know, maybe this was my chance to find out more information on Tag. Not that I was investigating. But maybe this could be my way of helping Mandee out. She may lack common sense, but that didn't mean she deserved to spend her future in prison for a crime she didn't commit.

I shifted, trying to look friendlier than I actually felt. "Speaking of Tag, what did he do for a living? Do you know?"

He pulled his head back, revealing several chins. "Of course, I know. We watch football together all the time. It gets me out of this apartment. I'm living with my mom right now while I'm on disability."

That explained why I hadn't seen him on Thursday when I questioned everyone at the apartment building. I'd talked to a sweet old lady who lived here. His mom.

"He's my friend." The man's voice caught. "He was my friend."

My heart panged with a moment of compassion. A man was dead. People mourned for him. And the loss was so senseless, at that. No one deserved to die at the hands—er, squeezing?—of a snake. Despite this man's off-putting manner, I could be cordial.

"I'm sorry for your loss," I said.

He swallowed hard, as if trying to compose himself, and waved his hand in front of his face as if embarrassed. "Thank you. Tag installed home security for Bunch Systems. He didn't love his job, but it was a paycheck. That's life sometimes, you know?"

"I understand. Any idea why he had manure on his feet?"

"Manure? What? No, I have no idea. Maybe he was installing security at a farm or something."

"Does he have family coming to make final arrangements?" The question had pressed on me. Were there people out there who cared about him? Who were mourning his death right now?

"Angel from upstairs told me that his mom is flying in from Washington State next week. He's all she has . . . had."

"I'm sorry to hear that." How awful for his mom. Losing her only son. All she had in the world. Reef's picture came to mind. Motherhood was really messing with my mojo lately. It was gradually altering my worldview, and, as a result, I felt off balance and uncertain. I wasn't used to feeling this way. "I realize this seems out of the blue, but did anyone dislike Tag?"

He stared me down, making it obvious that I was missing something. I had no idea what that might be until he said, "You mean, besides Patrick?"

I tried to remain neutral and not show my cluelessness. I hated being clueless. Absolutely hated it.

"Patrick didn't like him?"

The man smirked. "Tag threatened to turn Patrick in to Animal Control. He hated those snakes. Had a fear of snakes, for that matter."

If I'd been wearing a tight collar, I might have tugged on it. How was it possible that a man who hated snakes and who hated Patrick for having snakes had been killed by one of those very snakes? It was sadly poetic. "Did he?"

"He thought it should be illegal to keep so many in one apartment. He said it was inhumane, not to mention a safety risk for the other people who lived in this building. The two never quite saw eye to eye, and those snakes just added to the tension."

I nodded as I thought everything through. "It's a good thing Patrick wasn't in town. Otherwise, it sounds like he'd be the number one suspect."

The man flickered his eyebrows upward. "Yeah, I guess so. Or maybe he sent his minions to do his work."

"His minions?"

"That ditzy girl he had staying here. She'd be perfect for taking the fall. It looks like she did."

CHAPTER 6

"Reef is doing okay?" I repeated.

I'd already asked Chad twice as I sat in my car outside Patrick's apartment building. I trusted my husband. I really did. But no one knew Reef quite the way I did. I *had* carried him for nine months in my womb, which lent to my credibility.

"He's fine, Sierra," Chad said again. "Don't worry about us."

I could hear my baby cooing in the background, and my heart nearly melted. "But I know you have to work, and it's almost ten."

"Gabby actually said she'd watch him until two while I run to the hardware store. She's leaving later this evening to do a training workshop up in Delaware, but she said she has time until then."

Good old Gabby. If there was one thing I was certain about when it came to my friend it was that she'd fight with every last ounce of energy to protect the people she loved. Thank goodness, Reef was at the top of that list.

"Okay," I finally said. "If you're sure that everything's under control, I have a couple more things to do."

"With work or with your intern's trouble with the law?"

I frowned. "With Mandee. I just can't let this drop."

"Let what drop?"

I gave him an update on what I'd learned. He groaned toward the end. "That sounds like a mess, Sierra. You sure you want to get involved?"

"There's one thing I've learned over the past several months." I took a long sip of my water, feeling unusually dehydrated.

"What's that?"

I glanced at the picture of Reef I'd placed by my radio. "I fight for the lives of animals all the time, but humans should be included in that equation. Maybe at the top of it, for that matter. Just don't tell some of my coworkers because I might lose my job if they ever heard me admit that."

He chuckled. "I get it, and I'll keep that in mind. I think that's pretty wise of you, Sierra. It sounds like the girl needs help. Everybody needs somebody in their life who's willing to fight for them."

I hadn't been able to decide whether or not I should investigate who had access to the snake first or if I should investigate whether or not Tag had any enemies. I decided to start with Tag.

"I'm going to swing by the office of the guy who

died and see if I can find out anything," I finally said. "It's on my way to the bank anyway since I need to go there for work. By the way, do you know if Riley will be in tonight? I've been trying to call him, but he hasn't answered."

"I know he's working a lot of late days with this new law firm and he's been in court all week, but as far as I know he'll be home sometime this evening. Why?"

"Because I'm hoping he might represent Mandee. She can't go at this alone. She'll only make things worse for herself. I know he's busy, but it can't hurt to ask, right?"

"Ask Gabby. She'd tell you that asking questions can lead to *a lot* of trouble."

***

Bunch Systems was located in a strip of shops in Virginia Beach, in the shadow of a city park called Mt. Trashmore. The local landmark was a former trash dump that had been converted into a grass-covered hill—one of the only hills in the otherwise flat tidewater region of Virginia Beach. Located right off the interstate, it was quite the sight to see.

I parked in front of the business and hurried toward the front door. Inside, an older, grandmotherly looking woman sat behind the front desk laughing at something on the computer screen while she polished something in her hands. Was that a cane?

At first glance, I could easily imagine the woman

attacking someone with that very cane if they tried to break in to these facilities. I wasn't sure why I found it so mentally amusing that a security company had a grandmother out front, but I did. Maybe I'd expected a burly-looking guy with a badge and stun gun. Or maybe I was just so incredibly tired that my mind was going loopy on me. *That* was the more likely choice.

"What can I do for you?" When the woman spoke, I knew she was no joke. She may have looked small and sweet, but her voice held a dark side. It was gravelly, gruff, and almost menacing. She definitely had the "I was married to the mob, and I'm proud of it" vibe. It was a combination unlike any I'd ever seen before, and I was fascinated.

Or tired. Most likely tired.

"Well?" She didn't smile, only glared as she waited for my response.

I cleared my throat and approached the desk. "I was hoping to talk to a manager."

Ever so slightly, her eyebrow flickered upward in distrust. "About?"

"About Tag Wilson."

"Tag, huh?" Something shimmered across her gaze. "God rest his soul."

I nodded. "It's terrible what happened to him."

Her laser-like gaze remained on me. "Are you with the police?"

"No. But I have a few questions, if someone's willing to talk to me."

"I doubt anyone is."

The ease with which she brushed me off caused fire to ignite in my blood. I could be very persuasive when I needed to be. Like when animals were mistreated and I wanted people to see my point of view. Or when someone dismissed me. I hated being dismissed.

I tapped into that side of me now and nodded toward the limited green space out front. "Someone's dog has been defecating outside in front of the building for what appears to be weeks on end now," I started, playing on my powers of observation.

"What of it?"

"I do believe that's illegal. I can only assume, from both the feces and the smell of this building, that the dog is yours. Perhaps the manager would like to speak to me about that? I happen to know someone with Animal Control who would find that fact very interesting. He has a special fondness for people who forget to scoop the poop. The fines are . . . stinky, to put it lightly."

She pulled her chin back, as if my words had completely taken her off-guard. Finally, a smile cracked her wrinkled face, and she chuckled. "I like you. You've got guts and brains, and you're not afraid to use them. Good for you. Now," she slowly stood, "let me go see if I can find Brian."

I thought she would never reach the back hallway the way she shuffled there. But, eventually she did, and eventually a man came out. He was on the short side and had thick blond hair and a bushy mustache to match.

"Can I help you?" the man asked.

I raised my chin, wishing I'd had time to don a more professional outfit than my jeans and knit top. This moment really could use a power suit to up the pressure and my overall appearance. "Brian?"

He extended his hand, distrust lingering in his gaze. "The one-and-only Brian Bunch."

I shook his hand. "Sierra Davis. I'm looking into the death of Tag Wilson, and I was hoping you could help me."

"I thought you said you weren't with the police," the woman behind the desk quipped, her voice more scratchy and high-pitched with each word.

"I'm not."

"Then who're you working for?" she continued.

I let out a small sigh. "Do I need to remind you about the dog poop?"

She scowled and went back to polishing her cane, mumbling something incoherent under her breath.

"What can I help you with?" Brian said, looking slightly uncomfortable with my interaction with the woman I assumed to be his grandmother. I wasn't sure if he was afraid of me or of her, but my bets were on her.

"I was wondering if Tag had any problems with anyone here at work."

"Tag?" He blanched. "Why would you ask?"

"Because this is a criminal investigation. The police believe that a snake was purposefully set free in his apartment by someone with the intent to kill." I was overstating it a bit, but I didn't have time to waste words.

His eyes widened. "How . . . horrible. I have to be honest—I fired Tag last week. He was a nice enough guy. He even had my grandma and me over to eat a couple of times. But, the truth is, a lot of people here had problems with him, though I don't think anyone would kill him."

Now he had my attention. "Why did people have problems with Tag?"

He licked his lips before answering. "He was opinionated and hard to get along with. No one wanted to be on his team. Our clients complained about him. I gave him the chance to correct himself several times, but he was unwilling."

"Are you sure no one would want to kill him? It sounds like there were a lot of negative feelings, and negative feelings can lead to negative actions—actions like murder."

Brian raised his hands, probably mentally calculating the public-relations nightmare of my statement. It was enough to terrify any small-business owner. "Whoa. Slow down a minute. Those feelings didn't run *that* deep—not to my knowledge, at least."

I crossed my arms. "I'll be the judge of that."

"Let's be honest," Grandma yelled. "Tag Wilson was a lousy excuse for a human being. He didn't care about anyone else's feelings; he didn't care if he did a good job at work; and he felt entitled to get paid more than he was worth. I'm not saying I wanted the man to die, but I am saying that no one's going to miss him."

"Grandma. Please. This would be a great time for

you to play on the computer. Facebook is anxiously awaiting for your latest update." Brian shifted as he looked back at me. "Please ignore her. She thinks now that she's gotten up in years that she can say anything she wants any time she wants."

I actually kind of liked Grandma, but this wasn't the time to discuss it.

"Let me ask you this," Brian continued. "Maybe it can clear the air some. When did he pass?"

"Yesterday."

"My whole crew was up in Richmond working on a big job for a new mega jewelry store opening there. None of us were in town, and we all have alibis."

My heart sank a minute. I'd really hoped Brian might offer me a clue of some sort, but, if his words were true, that wasn't the case. "I see. Can you think of anything Tag mentioned that might give us an idea as to what happened?"

He drew in a long breath and stared off into the distance a moment. The early-morning sun crept in through the windows composing the front wall of the building and bathed the man in blinding brightness. "You know, now that I'm thinking about it, you might want to talk to Jim from Jungle Jim's."

"The pet shop?" Disgust dripped from my lips as I said the words. I'd opposed the shop many, many times for their treatment of animals. They viewed animals as products and merchandise instead of living beings, and I loathed them for it. They were at the top of my most-despised list.

"Yes, the pet shop. Last week, before I fired Tag, I caught him on the phone several times. He was talking with Jim, and it sounded rather heated. I asked Tag what was going on once, but he wouldn't tell me. I only know he looked ticked."

I nodded. I knew exactly whom I had to talk to next.

And maybe I could find a few pet store violations while I was there. That alone could redeem my day.

CHAPTER 7

Against my better instincts, I found myself at Jungle Jim's twenty minutes later, after I'd swung by the bank. I spotted Jim Benson right away by the aquariums and fish. The fifty-something man was short and on the thicker side. He'd always reminded me a tad of a monkey, mostly because his lips seemed to overly extend themselves as he spoke.

At the moment, he was directing some of his employees on how to properly clean the tanks, and he looked none too happy about it.

"The directions on the bottle are simple. One drop for every gallon. Not a whole capful just because you feel like it! Do you know what an overabundance of chemicals can do to these fish?"

Aw, he actually sounded like he cared about the quality of life for my finned friends.

"Too many chemicals can mean my inventory goes down the drain—literally. We'll be flushing these guppies by evening."

Any hopes I had that the man might be good and decent disappeared. Inventory? He called his fish *inventory*?

If I believed in reincarnation—which I didn't—I might hope he returned to this world as one of the very fish he mistreated.

At that moment, he looked up and saw me. Instantaneously, he scowled, shoved the chemicals into the quivering hands of one of his employees, and stormed toward me.

"Sierra Nakamura. For what do I have the pleasure of seeing you here today?" he sneered. Literally sneered.

"It's Sierra Davis now." I decided to get right to the point. "Do you know Tag Wilson?"

He sneered again. "Another one of my favorite people. How fortuitous that the two of you know each other."

"I don't actually know Tag. At least not in his living and breathing state."

"Huh?"

"He's dead," I announced as an aquarium gurgled beside me.

Jim's eyebrows shot up. "Dead? What happened?"

"A snake got to him." I watched his expression carefully, trying to determine if he had any clue about that fact before I told him.

His eyebrows slowly lowered back to normal position, yet his eyes retained a shocked expression. It appeared he was telling the truth—or he was a really great actor.

"I see," he finally said. "I heard a story on the news this morning about a man who died because of a python. I'm sorry to hear that was Tag."

"What were the two of you fighting about?"

A crease formed between his eyes, and his shock appeared to turn into irritation. "Who said we were fighting?"

"His former boss at Bunch Systems. Said it was quite heated. Plus your reaction when I said his name shows that he was not one of your favorite people."

His shoulders hunched up in overzealous outrage, and I expected at any minute he'd start treating me like his poor, defenseless little fish. I'd put my foot down as soon as he threatened to flush me. "What's this have to do with Paws and Fur Balls?"

"It's Animal Protective Services now, and that's none of your business. Now, would you please answer my questions before I report a number of violations I see here to the Better Business Bureau, and APS focuses their next campaign on you?"

He scowled. "There's nothing to report here, lady."

He obviously hadn't learned yet that I had an eagle eye for any type of violation concerning the well-being of animals. "I'll have you know that the Pet Purchase Protection Act deems it necessary—and mandatory—to display breeding history, as well as medical backgrounds, on the cages of the animals you're selling here."

"What of it?"

"When I walked past the puppies, I noticed you're not following that regulation. Just think of the fines you'll face if the wrong person finds out you're violating this act."

He shrugged again before narrowing his eyes. "Fine. Since you're going to play dirty—Tag and I had a disagreement. That's all. No big deal."

"A disagreement about . . ."

His eyes narrowed even farther. "A snake."

Now he had my interest. "What kind of snake?"

"A python I agreed to sell to one of his neighbors."

Say what? Certainly I hadn't heard him correctly. What sense did that make? "Why were you fighting with Tag about a snake that wasn't his?"

He grunted, grabbed a syphon, and started to vacuum the dirt from a tank full of guppies, probably so he could avoid eye contact with me. "Tag was trying to convince me to say that this snake was too dangerous for a residential area."

"And?"

He shrugged, syphoning out water like his life depended on it. "He almost had me swayed."

"What do you mean?"

He paused, his jaw tightening. "Apparently the guy who bought the snake liked to drape some of his snakes over his shoulders and walk around the apartment building. That's not smart snake ownership."

"You can't own animals—" I started, so tired of trying to persuade people to change their way of thinking.

It was an uphill battle.

"Yeah, yeah. I know. Save your argument for someone else. Anyway, Tag wanted me to sign a document saying the python was a public threat. He was going to take it to Animal Control and try to have the snake taken away."

I was trying to follow the logic here, but it seemed so convoluted. "So, it was okay for his neighbor Patrick to have the snake in his home as long as he didn't walk around with it over his shoulders in public?"

Jim sighed. "People think they can handle a snake that big, but most people can't. I began having second thoughts after I sold the snake. Nightmares, actually. I didn't want anything to happen. It looks like the worst-case scenario came true, though. I hate to hear that."

"Why even sell snakes like that at all if they're so dangerous?"

He paused from cleaning the fish tank, the water vacuum dripping all over the floor instead of into the bucket designed to catch the water. Jim didn't seem to notice or care. "I gotta make a living. It may not be the way you think I should, but it pays my bills. I got the snake from a man down in Carolina. A lot of people who have pythons get them at a young age so they're more moldable. This was a full-grown python, and we didn't know what the animal's history was. You have to know what you're doing in order to handle a snake of that size."

"Yet you sold it anyway?"

"I did, though I had misgivings. Patrick was very

convincing."

"How did Tag even get you involved in the first place? What made him call you of all people instead of going straight to Animal Control himself?"

Jim raised his shoulders. "We were friends. It's best to keep the government out of things."

"But you and Tag were fighting?"

"Only because Tag realized Patrick was never going to sell the snake back to me and he wasn't happy about it. Can you blame the guy?"

I sighed. It looked like the conversation hadn't gotten me anywhere.

***

At lunchtime, despite my determination to let it go, I ran over to Patrick's apartment again. I couldn't stop thinking about everything I'd learned this morning, and the questions I'd formed were hunting me like a hungry wolf after a long, desolate winter. Since Gabby had said she'd keep Reef until two, I needed to do this now.

I wanted to look at that vent one more time. I didn't know why. Honestly, I mostly wanted to figure this out so I could go on with my life. It was probably selfish of me, but, if I could knock things off my to-do list, maybe my level of stress would be reduced.

Stress reduction sounded like a great plan, especially considering that I'd snapped at two of my employees today and nearly chewed Chad out when he'd mentioned he forgot to change Reef's diaper. Now I hoped my sweet boy didn't get diaper rash. That would be just my luck, especially since Chad was leaving for West Virginia tomorrow, and he'd probably be gone for two weeks, at least.

Someone was standing at Patrick's door when I glanced up as I walked into the building. I bristled faster than a cat seeing a bathtub full of water. The young man— he was probably college-aged and he looked the role because of the stack of books and papers in his hands— looked down at me and offered a tight smile.

"Excuse me, ma'am. Do you live in this building?" He said the words quickly and succulently.

I shook my head as I climbed the stairs, boosting my bag higher on my shoulder. I'd upgraded my sling purse to a large tote that had room for diapers and wipes, and I was still getting used to it. "No, I don't. Can I help you with something?"

His eyebrows came together, and he frowned as I approached. "I need to drop off some homework for Patrick, and I haven't been able to get in touch with him."

"That's going to be difficult since he's in Costa Rica this week."

He squinted in confusion before shrugging so fiercely that it seemed over the top. "In Costa Rica? Why do you think he's in Costa Rica?"

"Patrick won a contest, and now he's vacationing in the rain forest."

The guy's nostrils flared as if the very idea was

CHRISTY BARRITT

repulsive. "Why would he be down there now?"

I was feeling a mix of curious and annoyed. I'd felt a lot of that since starting this unofficial investigation. "I don't know. Why not?"

He shrugged a little too adamantly. This guy was obviously tightly wound and thought I should be able to read his mind. His body language screamed "high-strung."

"Because Patrick has school," he said. "You don't just leave in the middle of the semester, especially not senior year."

In terms of reasoning, the notion wasn't solid enough to hold up in court. "Just because you wouldn't, that doesn't mean he wouldn't."

The student stared back at me like I'd grown a third eye. And like I was old and set in my ways. Little did he know that I'd been like this since before I hit puberty.

I nodded to the book in his hands. "So Patrick asked you to bring his schoolwork by?"

"No, but I know he needs this for one of our classes. He didn't show up this morning, so I thought I'd bring his assignments by. You know—I'm trying to be a good friend."

"Really?"

He scowled, caught in a lie. "We're actually partners for one of the assignments. If he doesn't do his part, that means I have to do it for him, or we both get marked down. I took Patrick as someone more responsible than this, and I resent him putting me in this position."

Now things were starting to make more sense.

76

"When exactly did you talk to him last?"

"Two days ago."

I tried not to show my surprise this time. "Let me get this straight: Two days ago you actually talked to Patrick? On the phone or in person?"

The guy looked uber-annoyed now. I assumed he hadn't guessed this conversation would be extended like this. After all, he'd started with a simple question. "That's right. I talked to Patrick. In person. Two days ago in Norfolk."

Patrick had lied to Mandee. But why? It just didn't make sense.

"That can't be right," I muttered.

He shoved the papers into my hands. "If you know so much about him, you give him these books. I've got to get to my next class."

"Wait! Where did the two of you meet two days ago?"

"At a coffeehouse in Norfolk. The Grounds. Now I've got to run."

CHAPTER 8

I wanted to go to The Grounds, but first I had to see Reef. Like, I *had to* had to. The longest I'd been away from him since he'd been born was seven hours. I was nearing that record now, and he was all I could think about.

When I walked into my apartment, Gabby was there, cradling Reef in her arms and studying some type of criminal justice handbook as he slept.

"You're going to spoil him," I told her.

She shrugged. "Is that a bad thing?"

I didn't say anything. Instead, I peered at his little face and felt myself relax. He was okay. Happy. Content. Cared for.

I had to grab a bite to eat or I was going to pass out. Luckily, my apartment was small enough that I could be in the kitchen and still easily talk to Gabby as she sat in the living room.

I put together a cucumber and sprout sandwich—I offered Gabby one, but she declined—and then I filled my friend in on my day.

"So, you've got to look at a couple of different things here," Gabby told me, closing her book. "First: who would want this guy dead? Second: who knew about the snakes? Third: who had access to the snakes? That would be a great start at finding your suspect."

I grabbed my sandwich and a glass of water as I thought her questions through. "Well, apparently a lot of people didn't like this Tag guy. I don't know if that means they would kill him, though."

"You might be surprised at people's motivations for committing terrible crimes. People blow situations up in their minds. I cleaned this crime scene once where a woman had been murdered. It turned out she'd just gotten divorced, and she'd gotten ownership . . . uh— custody, I mean—of the dog. As a result, her ex thought she was the devil. He killed her, got the dog back, but ultimately ended up in jail."

"I love animals, but . . . that's awful." I shuddered and sat down in the rocking chair across from her. I desperately wanted to hold Reef, but I didn't want to wake him up, and I knew I needed to eat while I had the chance.

"Tell me about it. People's perception of reality can be whacked-out. Anyway, who knew about the snake?" She leaned back into the couch, careful not to wake Reef.

I thought about her question a moment. "Everyone in the apartment building. People at the pet shop, I suppose. Maybe a few of his friends. Again, it doesn't really help me narrow down the suspects."

She nodded slowly. "Who had access to his apartment?"

"Mandee." I frowned when I said her name. Just the thought of her brought up negative feelings. "The landlord, I suppose. I'm not sure who else. However, Patrick's spare key was beneath his doormat. Anyone could have found it."

"True that." She sighed and squinted in thought. "The thing I find suspect here is that Patrick is supposedly in the area still. Why would he lie about that? Why would he want Mandee to snake-sit?"

"Maybe so Mandee would take the fall for him?" I suggested.

"It's that, or he's got impeccable timing," she said.

"Speaking of all this—I've been trying to catch up with Riley. I take it he's been busy lately?"

She nodded. "Big trial. It should be over soon. He's waiting for the jury to come back with their decision. Why?"

"I'm hoping he might help Mandee out."

"I'm sure he will. I'll mention it to him when I see him later."

I continued eating, letting my thoughts turn over. But that was all they were doing—they weren't going anywhere. Maybe I just needed to clear my head in order for more answers to come to light.

I knew the perfect subject change. I took the last bite of my sandwich—I'd finished it in a mere six bites. I really *had* been famished. Then I launched into a new set of questions.

"How are things between you and Riley, by the way?" I asked. "Did you set a date yet?"

She flinched. The action was so subtle that I almost missed it, but I knew her well enough to read her body language. "Not yet. I'm just enjoying the moment. It's when I start dreaming about the future that things get out of whack."

"What's that mean?"

She shrugged. "I don't even know what I mean. I suppose I'm saying that I'm going to take life day by day and enjoy what I've got while I've got it."

"That's . . . interesting." I wasn't sure where she was going with that thought. I wanted to ask her more about it, but, before I could, she stood.

"Speaking of the future . . . I've got to get ready for my trip."

I took Reef from her, and he continued sleeping against me.

Gabby straightened her clothes, wiping at some spit-up on her snarky "Everything's Better with Bacon" T-shirt. Since I didn't approve of bacon, I decided to pretend it was tofu bacon she was endorsing. I only choose the "ignorance is bliss" method for friends.

"I'll be gone a couple of days, come home, and then get ready to head to West Virginia to help Chad," Gabby continued.

"You're one busy girl." Just as I finished my sentence, Reef's eyes popped open. I smiled down at him.

"I'm excited about this old theme park we'll be restoring. It should be a lot of fun. And you know what they say about fun."

"No, what?"

"That girls just want to have it." She started singing the Cyndi Lauper song until I actually giggled. Well, Reef smiled first, and then every tense muscle in my body turned to gelatin.

"He smiled!" I said, my voice lilting with delight.

"Aunt Gabby will make you smile a lot," she said, giving him her best duck lips and waving her finger near his belly until he smiled again.

"You've got the touch," I told her.

"I'm telling you: you should come to West Virginia. It will be . . . fun. And I'll get to see Reef . . . and you too, of course. That's a given."

I raised my eyebrows. "Fun is not what I would call it."

"You can work from there. Come on. It would be like old times. The gang would be together again, living an adventure instead of going through the daily grind. Think about it. Life has been awfully adult-like lately."

Reef cooed in my arms again. Getting away did sound nice. So did hanging out with Gabby, Riley, and Chad. "I'll think about it."

"And keep me updated on this mystery. You know I'd love to dig in—if I didn't already have these workshops planned. Otherwise, I'd be right by your side."

I nodded. Her words were true. She was always

more than ready to jump in feet first. "Got it."

But first things first: I had to visit The Grounds.

***

The Grounds just happened to be located right across the street from my apartment building. I lived in a converted old Victorian in a trendy neighborhood located snugly beside downtown Norfolk. Everything I needed—and more—was located within walking distance of my home.

I planned on heading over there, but first I called into the office and gave various instructions to my employees about what to do, feeling the strange need to mention to everyone that I would be working this weekend. I didn't want anyone to think I was a slacker.

Then I put Reef into a sling, hurried across the street, and stepped into my favorite coffeehouse and hangout. The place was soothing, with its wood floors and eclectic table-and-chair sets. Local artwork hung on the walls, and acoustic music made everything better as it crooned through the speakers.

Sharon, the owner, called hello when I walked in. Then she immediately came over to see Reef. Story of my life lately, and I loved it.

Sharon had ever-changing hair color and multiple piercings all over her face, and she dressed with an edge— to put it lightly. But, despite her rough appearance, she was one of the kindest people I knew. Her niece Clarice even worked for Chad.

After a few minutes of chitchat, I got down to business. "Sharon, did you see this guy in here a few days ago?"

I'd gotten a picture of Patrick from his social media page—which he hadn't updated in a week. I thought that was strange because, before that, he'd updated it several times a day. Something must have happened to make him stop.

Anyway, I'd taken a screenshot on my phone so I could show it around.

Sharon paused from washing some blenders and measuring cups and studied it a moment before nodding. "Yeah, I've seen him in here before."

"Remember anything about him?"

She dipped her hands into the soapy water of her deep, stainless-steel sink. "He was talking with some guy in the corner last time he was here."

"When was that?"

"A couple of days ago."

"A couple of days ago? Like, literally a couple or figuratively?"

She looked back and smiled. "Yes, two actual days. What's going on? You sound like Gabby, asking all of these questions."

I shrugged, trying to sound casual. "I'm doing some research for a friend of mine. Did this guy seem pretty normal while he was here?"

She shrugged before rinsing the blender with steaming hot water. "I'd say so."

RATTLED

"Yet you remember it. All of the people who come in here, and you remember him?"

"It wasn't because of that I remembered him. It was because of what happened next."

"What happened?"

She paused from cleaning the dishes and turned toward me, her apron blotched with water. "The first guy he was talking with left, and then someone else came in. It was very confrontational. The two of them raised their voices, and I had to ask them to leave, actually."

"Do you know what they were arguing about?"

As if she couldn't resist working, she took her rag and began wiping the countertops. "It sounded like money, but I can't be sure. The other guy said something about a thousand bucks that was rightfully his."

"What did this guy look like?"

"I can do better than describing him. I heard his name. I only remember because it was so strange."

"What was it?"

Her eyes connected with mine. "Tag."

CHAPTER 9

I worked from home for a couple of hours before fixing vegetarian lasagna. Chad would be leaving the next day for his trip, so I wanted to make him something on the nicer side and not just soup, salad, or a sandwich.

As soon as we finished eating, my phone rang again. I almost didn't answer when I saw it was the jail. I knew what that meant: Mandee was calling again.

"I'm going to ignore it," I told Chad.

"Don't be silly. Answer."

I blinked at him. "Are you sure?"

"Of course."

I pushed aside my guilt over neglecting my family and scooted my chair out. "Excuse me a minute." I walking toward the bedroom for some privacy and put the phone to my ear to accept the collect call. "Hello?"

"Sierra? Can you come down to the jail? I need to talk with you. Please."

"Is this about your bail hearing?"

"My what?"

"I did some research online earlier, and, from what I understand, you should get a hearing within forty-eight hours of being booked. However, that's going to bring you right up until Sunday, and I'm pretty sure Sundays are excluded from that. It could be as late as Monday."

"What does all of that mean?"

I sighed. "Nothing. What are you calling about?"

"I need to see you."

"About . . . ?"

"I need to know what's going on! I'm going crazy in here, Sierra. I feel like everyone has forgotten about me."

Compassion panged at my heart again. "No one has forgotten about you. In fact, I've been running around all day today trying to find information for you."

"Please, come here and tell me what you found out."

I glanced back at the table where Chad finished eating his dinner while cradling Reef. "We can do it over the phone."

"Please, Sierra. I really need to see a friendly face. I've never felt so alone in my life, and you're the only one I can talk to."

I almost wanted to call her out on her constant demands, but I didn't. She had enough on her mind without me reprimanding her. "I'll see what I can do."

Everything was always urgent for Mandee. Although, in this case, she was in jail, so maybe it really was urgent.

Guilt continued to pound at me as I made my way

back toward the table. "I'm so sorry—"

"Let me guess: She needs you?" Chad looked away from Reef long enough to watch my reaction.

I nodded. "She sounds desperate."

"She probably is. Go."

"Are you sure?"

"Absolutely. We'll be fine. Besides, it will be nice to spend some time with Reef before I leave. You know, father-and-son bonding. You can never get too much of that."

Relief filled me. "Thank you. I'll make this up to you somehow."

"Don't be silly. Just go. The sooner you get there, the sooner you can come home. Right?"

I nodded. "Right."

***

In the little visiting area at the jail, with a piece of glass between us, I finished filling Mandee in on what I'd learned today. Then I had some questions for her.

I got right to the point, determined not to let Mandee get me off track—again. "Did you know Patrick was in town?"

Her eyes widened through the glass partition separating us. "No, he's not."

"He is. I have eyewitnesses who not only spoke with him but who met with him."

Her entire body seemed to slump toward the table

in front of her. The poor girl already looked pale and had huge circles under her eyes after only one day here. This was going to be a rough ride for her.

"He told me he was going to Costa Rica," she said.

"Is there any reason he would lie?"

She thought about it and then shook her head.

"No. I mean, why would he?" She seemed to realize how that might tie in with this murder investigation, and her eyes widened again. "Unless . . ."

I raised a hand to halt her thoughts. "We don't know anything yet. I just find it suspicious that Patrick is keeping some kind of secret."

She frowned, a hint of despair creeping into her gaze. "You're not the only one."

"Tell me about Patrick," I prodded.

She let out a long sigh, her fingers nervously tousling each other atop the table. "Patrick . . . he's—he's great. He loves kayaking. And animals. And he wants to be a photographer. Those are his pictures on the walls at his apartment. He's really good."

I'd seen the pictures, and I was prone to agree. He had an eye for visually pleasing images.

"What's he studying at school?" I asked.

"Engineering."

"Was he working anywhere?"

"Not that I know of. Then again, we were out of touch for a while," Mandee said.

"Do you realize that he supposedly won a contest on the back of a cereal box but there's no cereal in his apartment?"

"Maybe he threw them all out before I came."

I shrugged. "Maybe. It just seems weird. I've never actually known anyone who's won one of those 'win a free trip' things."

"I guess it was all a lie." She shook her head and lowered her entire upper half toward the desk as if her burdens were great. "I just don't understand any of this. It doesn't make sense. It doesn't fit the person I know Patrick to be."

It doesn't fit who you want him to be. I kept that thought silent. "Do you have his cell phone number?"

"Of course."

As she said it aloud, I committed it to my memory. I'd had to deposit my phone and purse into a locker before coming in, so I had no other choice.

"Why did he ask you to take care of his animals instead of someone else?"

She shrugged, like she hadn't given it a second thought. "Because he knows I'm an animal lover."

"And you only knew him for a few months?"

"That's correct. We met on the crew team."

I had the feeling she thought more of Patrick than he thought of her. Maybe he thought she'd be the perfect sucker or scapegoat or both. "And you remained in touch?"

She nodded. "Kind of. I mean, we ran into each other at school a couple of weeks ago and kind of reconnected. I was surprised when he called me out of the blue to ask me if I'd stay over at his place. He said it was all last minute and that he knew I loved animals."

I nodded. I supposed the story could be valid. Still, Patrick remained on my radar. I didn't trust him yet. "Do you know of any other friends of Patrick's I could contact with questions?"

She shrugged again. "I'm sure he has other friends. I just don't know any of them."

"How about the other guys from the crew team?"

"They all graduated, and I have no idea where they ended up. I definitely don't have their contact info. Only Patrick's."

I nodded, trying to remember each of these details so I could use them for future reference. My memory hadn't been quite as good as it used to be. I was pretty sure Reef had stolen a good chunk of my brain cells. Before thus-said brain cells were stolen, I would have tried to intellectually explain my dilemma by saying something like: pregnancy hormones had primed and reshaped my brain. Now I just called it "Mommy Brain." "Anything else you should tell me?"

Mandee frowned, just not looking like the same Mandee in the drab jail garb. "I'm going to spend the best years of my life here, aren't I?"

"Not if I have anything to do with it."

***

Even though I felt like I was on a wild goose chase, I

headed back to Patrick's place. I had too many questions and not enough answers. It was my third time there today, but, thankfully, it was right down the street from mine. It was already nine o'clock, and I hoped to head home after this.

What had started as doing something out of obligation for Mandee had turned into a quest for the truth.

I found the extra key under the doormat and slid it into his lock before slipping inside. Somewhere in here there had to be answers. Why would Patrick be in town but tell Mandee that he wasn't? What purpose could that serve?

Unless he wanted her to look guilty for a crime she didn't commit. Was Mandee's friend really that desperate? Was he heartless enough to set her up?

If there was any place to find answers, it was in his apartment—so that's exactly what I planned on doing: looking through his things in order to find a clue.

Had Patrick been back since he supposedly left? Was there any evidence that would show what he was really doing in town? Any correspondence that might indicate a rift between him and Tag?

I stepped into the apartment, closed the door, and paused. Where did I even start?

His desk, I decided.

It was tucked into the corner of the living room, and going through the papers there should win me some kind of special honor. His desk was atrocious with papers piled high, as well as other clutter and trash. I had no idea what I might find under all of this. It could be something helpful or it could be something disgusting.

I opened the first drawer. It was full of envelopes, stamps, paperclips, and pens. Nothing exciting.

The next drawer contained old college assignments for his engineering classes.

Again—nothing exciting.

I went through three more drawers and still didn't find anything. Was all this for nothing?

I shoved some items on top of the desk out of the way. There were old food containers, dirty socks, and banana peels. Seriously gross.

Come on, Sierra. Think! Somewhere in this place there's evidence of where he is. There has to be. Everyone leaves some kind of paper trail.

I paused when I found a camera beneath a coffee-stained T-shirt. A camera? What could be on here?

I turned it on and began scrolling through pictures. Most of them were of wildlife. Birds and turtles and even a cottonmouth, all out in nature.

Thirty or so pictures in, I paused at the photo of two guys posing beside a kayak. One of them was Patrick. I recognized him from his Facebook page.

Kayaking? Mandee had said Patrick was on a crew team and that he enjoyed kayaking. I zoomed in on the picture until I could read the lapel of the guys' shirts.

Deepwater Kayaking.

What kind of connection did Patrick have with the

company? Did he work for them? That would be my guess based on his uniform.

First thing tomorrow morning, I was going to find out.

For now, I needed to be with my family.

And to sleep. I couldn't forget that.

CHAPTER 10

"Do you have to go?" I couldn't believe those words had just come out of my mouth. I usually wasn't the clingy type. But the thought of not seeing Chad for two weeks did something to me. It made me . . . sad.

Chad threw some toiletries into an oversized ziplock bag before plopping the whole thing into his suitcase. "You know I'd stay if I could. But this will be a good paycheck for us. It will go a long way toward saving money for that dream house we've been talking about finding."

"It's hardly a dream house we've been talking about," I reminded him, rubbing Reef's back as he rested on my shoulder. We just wanted something larger. With a backyard. And a swing set. It was more a matter of function than fantasy.

"I know. But it's getting a little cramped here."

"You really think you can finish this in two weeks?" I asked, following him as he pulled his suitcase from the bed and started toward the front door.

"I'm hoping I'll be able to. It's a big job. It will be a lot of work. But I have the rest of the crew meeting me there, plus I'm going to interview some subcontractors. That's why I'm going early. Nate is anxious to get this off the ground."

Nate Reynolds was his friend in West Virginia who'd hired him. He'd either bought or inherited an old theme park—I couldn't remember the exact details at the moment—but he was hoping to restore it as a resort destination where people could rent cabins and relive the old days.

"You should come." He paused by the door.

I shrugged. "I would. But I have a lot of work to do."

"Bring it with you. There are advantages to being the boss, you know."

I nodded slowly. "I'll think about it. It could be fun. We haven't gotten away . . . in a long time."

Chad leaned toward me and planted a firm kiss on my lips. "I'll miss you."

"I'll miss you too."

He kissed the top of Reef's head. "I'll miss this little guy too."

Reef cooed in response.

"Try to stay out of trouble," Chad reminded me. "I know you have a lot going on with Mandee. But pace yourself. Promise?"

I nodded. "Promise."

"I love you." He kissed me again.

"I love you too. Be safe."

* * *

As promised, I went to Deepwater Kayaking, arriving just as they opened—I'd checked the time on their website. After putting Reef in my sling, I paused outside my car and observed the business a moment.

It was located on a little inlet of water flowing from Back Bay. The building itself was built to look like a shack, even though it was new. Boards had been purposely nailed crooked, and the shutters were painted a bright turquoise.

Behind the building was a row of colorful kayaks, all lined up on end and leaning against an outdoor pavilion. Life jackets—orange, yellow, and blue—hung on a string between the main building and the pavilion.

Beyond all of that, where the water met the land, there was a small pier surrounded by marsh grass.

All in all, this looked like a lovely way to spend a day. Other people obviously thought so also, because customers were already here and being fitted for life jackets by the water.

I took a step toward the main building. I'd dressed down in order to look more legit. I figured no one would take me seriously if I was wearing a business suit—not here, at least.

I walked inside and scanned the faces there for Patrick. I didn't see him—I'd figured it couldn't be that easy. There was a counter at the back where two guys checked people in. A video ran on a TV overhead, advising people on kayaking and water safety instructions. On the walls were wetsuits and paddles and other equipment people could purchase.

A guy who looked like he could be friends with Chad approached with a clipboard in his hands. He had shaggy hair and looked like he lived in his orange bathing suit and that he'd be naked without his tan.

"Can I help you? I must say, we don't do very many tours with babies." He awkwardly peered into the baby carrier and frowned at Reef.

I'd come up with a cover story on my way here. "Oh, I'm not here about a tour. Not a new tour, at least. I'm here about an old one I did, though. I was hoping you could help me."

"Sure thing. What do you need?" He shifted his clipboard from his right hand to his left side.

"It's my tour guide."

The man frowned, as if expecting bad news. "Uh oh."

"It's not that. It's that I forgot to tip him. I wanted to apologize to him." The lie rolled off my lips so easily that I almost squirmed. I wasn't in favor of lying, but I was desperate for answers—not that that should justify it.

His shoulders visibly relaxed. "I'm sure I can leave some money and a note for him."

I forced a frown, sure it looked fake, but I pressed on regardless. "I'd really like to talk to him face-to-face, if at all possible."

He looked up at a new group of people who'd just entered. He'd probably rather be helping them than wasting time with me. I couldn't let that happen.

"Well, who was your guide?" he asked, his gaze still flickering behind me.

"Patrick . . . Something."

The man's smile disappeared. "Patrick, you said? How long ago was this tour exactly?"

"During the summer. July maybe. Why?"

The man nodded slowly, flashing a bright smile to a particularly cute blonde who walked past and looked his way. "Patrick is back at college and not working for us anymore."

I frowned again. "Oh, that's too bad. I was hoping he was still here. I was thinking about bringing my company here on another tour, but only if he led it."

The man shifted, and I had a feeling he was going to abandon me any time now in favor of the leggy blonde. "Unfortunately, he's not going to be able to do that. We were hoping he could continue with us part-time. He even said he would try to help out until we closed for the season. But he changed his mind last week. I guess his school workload was too much. But I'm sure we can plug you in with someone else. Someone who will be just as good."

I leaned closer. "I know that has to be a loss for you guys. He was so good."

He shrugged. "Funny that you said that. You're actually the second person who's come here looking for him this week."

I raised an eyebrow. "Am I?"

"Yeah, these other guys came in a few days ago. Kind of rough looking. They said they wanted Patrick to give them a tour also, but I didn't believe a word they said. They looked like they were up to no good."

Maybe I was finally on to something! "That's . . . crazy. You'd never seen them before?"

The man shook his head. "No, I haven't."

"Well, let me just be honest for a moment." I leaned even closer, as if sharing a secret. "I actually want to buy one of Patrick's photos. I thought they were beautiful. I wasn't sure if he was allowed to talk about selling them while he was on duty here, so I didn't want to get him in trouble."

Realization lit the man's face. He seemed to fall for my excuse. "I get it now. Yeah, he does take some really good photos. I get that."

"You know how I can get in touch with him?"

"Well, obviously I can't give you his home address. That would be weird. But I can tell you that he volunteers with that homeless shelter in downtown Norfolk once a week. Maybe you can catch him there."

It wasn't much to go on, but at least it was something.

I turned to leave but paused. "One more thing. Are you sure it was his college schedule that made him quit? He just seemed to enjoy his job so much."

The man shrugged. "No, it was kind of weird. One

day he was happy as a clam and said his schedule here looked great. The next day, he appeared kind of shaken. He said he couldn't do this anymore. I asked why, but he didn't say anything. I wondered if he was in some kind of trouble."

Some kind of trouble. That sounded about right. "Thanks for your help."

"No problem. I hope you find him."

"Me too," I whispered. "Me too."

***

Since I had no means of tracking down the rough looking men who'd stopped by trying to find Patrick, that left me with the homeless shelter. It was a long shot, but I decided to try anyway.

A theory had begun to form in my mind. Patrick was hiding from something. What were people who disappear trying to avoid, though? An ex-girlfriend? Maybe. Bill collectors? It was a possibility. The Mafia? It happened in the movies.

I pulled up to the homeless shelter located in downtown Norfolk in an old building that—if I remembered correctly—had been a luxury hotel in its early life. Today, this area of town had become less highbrow and more ghetto.

I walked through the front door, Reef strapped across my chest. The place had a peculiar smell—then again, I was always sensitive to scents. I smelled bacon, vanilla-scented air freshener, and dirty clothes, and I'd only made it as far as the administrative area.

A college-aged girl sat at the front desk and smiled at me. "Can I help you?"

"I have a question about one of your volunteers. Is there someone who oversees them whom I can speak with?"

She smiled again. "One moment."

A few minutes later a later, a woman I guessed to be in her early fifties, emerged from a back hallway. She had mousy, brown hair cut in a short style that may have made her appear older than she was. Her dowdy, brown suit didn't help the look, but it did fit her tiny voice and almost timid actions.

She introduced herself as Karen, the volunteer coordinator.

I explained to her that I was looking for Patrick.

"As a matter of fact, Patrick has been here this week. He's been working the night shift for us," Karen told me.

She'd just told me that Patrick had been volunteering this week. Wasn't that interesting? "I'd really like to talk to him. Do you know if he'll be back tonight?"

She nodded as we stood in the entryway of the building near the administrative offices. "I believe so. He's been very dedicated."

Something about the way she said it raised a few red flags. "Is it unusual for him to be dedicated?"

She shrugged, wringing her hands together as if

nervous. "Well, I don't know if I would say that. He just said he had more time this week than usual. He's taking fewer classes this semester, which has opened up his schedule more. Is there any reason you're asking?"

I smoothed my shirt, hoping I didn't look as rumpled as Karen did. At least Reef was with me, so I'd looked like a harried mom instead of a frazzled twenty-something with no good excuse.

"I've been trying to get in touch with him, and one of his friends told me I should check here," I continued. "I thought it was worth a shot. It's not an emergency, but he's not answering his cell phone. I have to admit that I'm kind of getting worried."

The woman looked over my shoulder, and a flash of concern etched across her face. I followed her gaze and spotted three guys entering through the front door. Each wore a black leather jacket and had a scraggly beard. Before they even said a word, I realized they looked like trouble.

Trouble . . .?

Could these be the men the guy at the kayak store had mentioned? It was a theory worth visiting.

"Can I help you?" the woman called, stepping toward them.

"We're looking for a place to stay tonight," one of them said. He was the roughest looking of the bunch, with a salt-and-pepper beard that came all the way down to his belly. His skin was wrinkled, he had a gold tooth, and he wore a bandana over his hair.

"I'm sorry. We don't have any beds open right now."

He lowered his gaze. "But I'm desperate." His words fell flat and sounded anything but sincere.

"This shelter is only for the homeless, sir." The woman wrung her hands nervously. I felt bad for her. These guys were bullies, and this woman seemed exceedingly kind and soft-spoken.

"Who says we're not homeless?" the man said. The word "Viking King" was stitched into the front of his jacket. Another guy shifted, and I noticed the word "Viking" on his jacket as well.

"We have a pulse on the homeless community in this area. I've never seen you."

He practically growled. "Well, obviously, you haven't met everyone."

I stepped forward, sensing Karen's nervousness. "Sir, I believe she made herself clear. You're not welcome here."

The man definitely growled this time, and he leered toward me. "I don't believe we involved you in this conversation."

"I wasn't waiting for an invitation." My outspokenness had gotten me in trouble on more than one occasion.

The man's face turned even redder. "You don't know who you're messing with."

"I think I do."

The man looked at Karen then turned his gaze back

to me. The other woman's presence here right now may have been the only thing that allowed me to remain in one piece. Well, Karen and Reef.

"You better hope you never run into me again. Do you hear?"

"Oh, I hear you." I couldn't resist the quip. If there was one thing my tiger mom had taught me, it was not to back down to anyone. The skill had served me well in my career and through multiple animal rights campaigns. I just hoped it didn't backfire on me now.

Finally, the men left the way they came. Karen turned toward me when they were gone. "I'm so glad you were here, but I apologize you had to experience that."

I shrugged, like it happened every day. "It's okay. I don't like bullies."

She offered a grateful smile. "Come back again tonight if you're trying to catch Patrick. He said he'd be here at seven."

If he showed up at seven, he might, unfortunately, have other people waiting for him also. That was why I needed to find Patrick first.

CHAPTER 11

Reef and I headed to the office so I could work on getting caught up for a while. Usually, Saturdays were quiet days there, and I hoped today would be the same.

As soon as I walked in, I knew my hopes were dashed. I spotted three people gathered around a desk. An air of excitement surrounded them as they sifted through papers and shot off snippets of conversation. They'd brought their cats—we had an open-door policy for that. They all seemed content to spend the day here.

Chloe hurried toward me. "Did you see it?"

"See what?" I braced myself, feeling like I was missing something big.

"This!" She held up the newspaper. On the second page was an article about the euthanasia of Chalice, written on behalf of Animal Protective Services.

I swallowed hard and fought back irritation. Had I signed off on this? I couldn't remember.

I quickly scanned it. It was pretty much a scathing editorial written to Animal Control about the fact they were considering euthanizing a nonaggressive animal who'd followed its instincts.

"I also started a campaign on social media for 'Animal Lives Matter.' It's spreading like wildfire." Chloe's eyes were blazing with that very wildfire. She felt passionate about this.

The image of Tag's lifeless body flashed through my mind.

It wasn't Chalice's fault.

I tried to tell myself that. And, at heart, I believed it. But did I think she should be sold to the next person who wanted a snake like that?

No. That snake didn't belong in someone's home. Most people weren't experienced enough to know how to handle her.

On one hand, there was the importance of saving an animal's life. That was vital. But, at times, we also had to think about public safety. I didn't want to see animals *or* humans being mistreated.

"Well? What do you think?" Chloe waited for my response.

"It looks like you've made a splash." I looked at the newspaper article again and hesitated. "Did I approve this?"

Chloe narrowed her eyes. "You signed off on it. Would you like to see your signature on the paperwork?"

I shook my head. "No, I believe you."

"What's wrong?"

"I'm just not sure this is the campaign we should

try to make the biggest waves with, not when there are so many other worthy causes out there."

Her bottom lip dropped open. "Every animal's life matters. Don't you agree? It doesn't matter if they're sweet and cuddly or slithery and slimy or tiny and considered a nuisance."

"I don't disagree." Reef started to stir, and he wasn't happy. A peculiar—yet familiar—smell filled the air. He'd soiled his diaper, I realized.

"Then why are you hesitant?"

I tried not to breathe through my nose and to keep my expression neutral. But certainly everyone else could smell the vile scent coming from us. "I think this issue is complex."

She crossed her arms. "Well, what do you want me to do?"

I let out a sigh, realizing I was dealing with an earlier version of myself. I would have reacted this exact same way a few months ago. But I felt like I was undergoing some kind of mental crisis right now.

"It's because Mandee is involved, isn't it?" Chloe gave me a sharp look. I knew she wasn't meaning any disrespect. It was just that her passion had bubbled to the surface. "I heard it through the grapevine."

"It's because the animal killed someone."

"But—"

"I know." I needed to nip the argument in the bud. "But that snake is a danger to anyone who doesn't know how to handle her."

The fire in her eyes was now directed at me. "I thought better of you."

"Chloe, this doesn't mean that I don't love animals and want to look out for their wellbeing. I'm just saying this is complicated and shouldn't be taken lightly."

She held up the newspaper. "Well, now everyone in this area knows our stance on the issue."

"I understand." I was well aware of that. But I didn't have time to get into all the intricate details at the moment. Reef was squirming, he smelled terrible, and I needed to change his diaper before it leaked through the fabric carrier and onto my shirt.

Gross.

"I don't think you do. This was only part one. The second part of my editorial will run tomorrow. People continue to share the memes I made for social media. We're having a protest outside of Animal Control on Monday."

I blinked. "You really went all out, didn't you?"

"Did you expect anything less?"

"No, of course not." Reef's cries became more agitated. "I don't know what to say. I'm going to have to think this through."

"Well, we don't have much time, so I hope you'll make this top priority." She scrunched her nose. "And please, for the sake of every living and breathing being, change that diaper."

***

I stayed at the office three more hours before closing up for the day. I'd begun trying to delegate a lot of the big campaigns we had. It had started when I took my maternity leave, and there was no reason it couldn't carry over into the future. Though I needed to approve many of the tactics before they went live, that was a lot less tedious than trying to plan everything myself.

However, in doing so, things like today's situation were going to pop up. It was impossible to have control over each detail of each campaign. I needed to put people in charge whom I could trust, and then I needed to release them to do the job they'd been hired to accomplish.

I was going to have to learn boundaries, which was hard for me since for most of my adult life I'd poured every part of my being into fighting for the rights of animals. Then Chad and I married, and that changed my priorities. Now Reef was here, and I didn't want to miss a single moment with him.

Right now, Reef and I were hanging out in the apartment and I was trying to get caught up on some household stuff like laundry. My mom had called. She called once a month and talked for twenty minutes each time. That was just the kind of mom she was.

She had come to visit Reef once when he was only a month old. I was shocked that she'd come for a visit, period. It had been her one and only time coming down here.

She'd ended our conversation by offering to give

Chad and me some money for a down payment so we could move into a more respectable area of town. Status was very important to my mother and father. They hated to see me live in this eclectic area where everything wasn't spic-and-span perfect. And now that they had a grandbaby, they *really* only wanted the best for their offspring.

As if she ever would have accepted money from her mother when she was my age. No way. My mom had worked sixty-plus hours a week when I was a child, and I'd gone through a slew of full-time nannies in the process.

If there was one thing I'd learned about my childhood, it was that I didn't want to replicate it for Reef. Sure, my mom had probably only been doing what she thought was best for me. But I'd been miserable. My animals had been the only things to comfort me, which is probably why I wanted to comfort them and return the favor now.

I'd just gotten off the phone with her when someone knocked at my door. My first thought was about the scary-looking motorcycles dudes I'd seen earlier. But they had no idea who I was or where I lived.

That didn't ease my nerves when I went to the door, though.

Thankfully, it was just Riley. He was tall and lean and had crystal-blue eyes. About a year ago, a criminal had shot him in the head, and none of us were sure he'd ever recover. He had, and he was back to his old self.

At the moment, he looked nothing like an attorney.

CHRISTY BARRITT

He wore dark, fitted jeans and a long-sleeve baseball T-shirt.

"I heard you wanted to talk. I was wrapping up a big trial and didn't have a chance to call you back. My apologies." He popped a peanut into his mouth as he stood in the doorway. "Sorry—this is my lunch today."

I nodded and let him inside. "Yeah, thanks for stopping by. I'd offer you something to eat, but I have nothing."

"I'm good. I'm doing a high-protein diet right now anyway as part of my training."

"Mixed martial arts, right?"

He nodded. "Right. I'm entered in a tournament next month, so I've got to get focused with my training."

I closed the door and went back to the couch where I was folding clothes. I'd figured out they wouldn't magically fold themselves. At least I could talk to Riley and get some housework done. Multitasking was going to be my best friend for the next couple of weeks. Actually, for the rest of my life.

Riley paused by Reef, who lay in a little bouncy seat. He talked to him a few minutes and gently tickled his belly. Reef had always loved Riley. My blood relatives may not be close, but I was so glad for Gabby and Riley to fill in as aunt and uncle for my baby.

"Did Chad leave this morning?" He pulled out a chair at the dining room table and continued to eat his peanuts.

I nodded. "He did. He went a week early to get

permits and supplies and to secure some subs for the big job."

"Did Gabby tell you?"

"Tell me what?" Were they officially engaged? No, that couldn't be it. Certainly Gabby would have told me that by now.

"I'm heading over to West Virginia also. The big trial I've been working on wrapped up yesterday. I've been so busy that Gabby and I haven't had much time together lately. I'm going to go with her and help out. Besides, it seems like Chad can use all the help he can get."

"I can't argue that." He'd been downright stressed about it.

"You should go too."

"Funny—I think Gabby suggested that also." I folded another of Reef's many outfits. I had no idea that one little baby could produce so much laundry. It was a byproduct of spit-up and diaper emergencies.

"It would be fun. The gang hasn't had a chance to hang out very much lately."

"I'll think about it."

"Now, what did you want to see me about?" Riley crumpled his peanut bag and sent a basketball shot toward the trashcan. He made it.

"I have this situation . . ." I proceeded to tell him about what happened with Mandee and Chalice. He listened carefully as I shared each detail.

"That certainly sounds . . . interesting."

I nodded. "Doesn't it?"

"When's her bail bond hearing?"

"I'm not sure, but she hasn't had it yet. She was arrested around 3:00 a.m. on Friday, and this is the earliest they could get her before the judge."

"That stinks. Nobody likes to stay in jail that long—especially not the innocent."

"Yeah, I feel bad for her."

"I can probably help."

"She says she has no money."

"I'm not really worried about that. I'm more worried about how guilty she looks."

I nibbled on the inside of my lip for a moment. "You think she looks guilty?"

"It's like you said: Maybe she didn't intend to kill this guy. But she knew he hated snakes. She knew he lived beneath her. Her prints were on the crowbar that apparently was used to pry the vent away from the floor. She could have easily left the lid off the enclosure and waited to see what happened, having no clue this guy would die."

I fought a frown, unwilling to show defeat. "I don't think she would do something like that."

Riley let his head fall slightly to the side. "You said she's spacy. Maybe she didn't think everything through."

I couldn't argue that. "It's a possibility. But it turns out Patrick is actually in town. I think that makes him look guilty. I mean, I know a lot of people who love their animals—who love them enough to do whatever it takes to keep them. If this guy Tag was threatening to go to

Animal Control, maybe Patrick came up with the perfect scenario to silence him, all the while pointing the blame at Mandee."

"Sounds like an awful friend to have." He stood. "You mind if I get some water?"

"Go right ahead." I continued folding my laundry. "I think Mandee likes Patrick. He could have used her kindness to his advantage."

"There are people who will do that. Are the police investigating him?" He grabbed a glass and filled it with tap water from the sink.

I shrugged, wishing I had something to offer him. But I desperately needed to go grocery shopping. "I have no idea. I know they were trying to reach him, but he told Mandee he was going to be in Costa Rica and unable to be contacted by cell phone."

"Convenient. If the police aren't looking at someone else, then they're just focusing on Mandee. That's not good." He sat back down across from me again and took a long swig of his water.

"What should I do?"

He pulled the glass in front of him and wiped a stray drop of water away from his lip. "How about if I take over as legal counsel for you?"

Those were the words I'd been hoping to hear. "You'd do that?"

"Of course. That's what friends are for."

A grateful smile tugged at my lips. "Thanks, Riley. I really appreciate it."

"No problem. Now, enjoy your day off. I know you don't get very many of them."

CHAPTER 12

At six o'clock that evening, I packed up Reef and we headed to the homeless shelter. I really didn't want to bring my baby with me, but I had no other choice. All of my usual sitters were busy or out of town. Plus, who looked more unassuming than a woman with a baby?

I'd actually left early to make an evening of it. I'd gone to my favorite vegan restaurant, and Reef had slept against me in the sling while I read a new book. It was the first time I'd felt truly relaxed in months. However, the moment I started thinking about Mandee and the whole situation, tension filled me again.

It was time to nip all of this in the bud and head to the homeless shelter. I needed to catch Patrick and ask him some very specific questions.

There were three different places where people could park near the shelter: a parking garage across the street that also serviced some nearby restaurants; the street itself, which had a limited number of spots along the curb; and a small lot right behind the building for employees and volunteers.

I managed to grab a space on the street before positioning myself on the corner across the street, where I had a good view of all three areas.

Mandee had called again earlier. She'd gushed and gushed about meeting with Riley, who must have gone to the jail as soon as he left my place. Apparently, she thought he was handsome and that was the majority of what she wanted to chat about. I reminded her that Riley was dating my best friend, and that silenced her rather quickly.

Which allowed me to ask her my own pressing questions.

Mandee told me that Patrick drove a beat-up mauve Ford Ranger. I hadn't exactly explained everything to her. I didn't want word getting back to Riley or Chad about what I was doing.

I knew being here was risky, especially bringing Reef. That's why I'd vowed to remain in the background and play it safe, no matter the cost. I could handle putting my own life in danger, but never my son's.

Thankfully, the evening air was mild and the sun hadn't quite set yet, which left some daylight for me. Daylight always felt safer than darkness. I knew it wasn't logical, but it was true.

I gently pushed the stroller back and forth as I waited, pretending to play on my phone so I wouldn't look suspicious. Around 6:45, I finally saw a mauve Ford Ranger pull into the parking garage. A moment later, Patrick emerged from the exit. He nervously looked both ways on the sidewalk before starting across the street.

I took a step toward him but stopped in my tracks.

Just as I'd feared: the men I'd seen here earlier had returned, and they had vengeance in their eyes.

I paused, feeling pulled between helping someone who might be in trouble and ensuring that my son still had a mom after today. There was no way I could put Reef in danger.

So I did the only thing I could think of. I called Detective DePalma. I whispered how urgent the situation was. I begged him to come quickly. Then I slunk behind the corner, desperate to keep Reef out of sight.

As I stood there, I prayed. I prayed for Patrick. I didn't know if he was the good guy here or the bad guy. But I knew his life was on the line now.

I wasn't much of a pray-er. In fact, I'd just started going to church recently at Gabby's prodding. I'd grown up in a home with parents who'd emphasized self-reliance and who'd put faith only in the smartest humans and their discoveries in the fields of science.

But now that I had a child, I wanted more for him. I wanted him to believe there was more to this life than living for the moment. That there was hope beyond the realms of this world. That his life was for a purpose and by design.

Peeking around the corner, I held my breath as the men forced Patrick against the wall. There were three of them against only one skinny and slight Patrick.

He had no chance.

How in the world had he gotten entangled with these men?

The men began roughing him up. They shoved him. Poked him. Taunted him.

I couldn't make out what they said, but I thought I heard something about money.

Come on, Detective. You can get here any time now.

I gripped the stroller, rocking it back and forth as Reef let out a little coo. The coo turned into a cry.

Oh, no. No, no, no, no.

The cry turned into an all-out wail.

All four men turned their attention to me.

This wasn't good.

I ducked back behind the corner and glanced down the street. Could I start running with the stroller toward the restaurant in the distance?

Running with this stroller didn't seem safe. But neither did facing those guys.

I looked back and saw one of them start toward me. Recognition lit in his eyes.

"I'm so sorry, Reef," I whispered.

Then I took off, desperate to put distance between that man and my son.

Thankfully, even though the man was large, his footsteps were heavy and lumbered. He wouldn't easily catch up with me. But I still wasn't in the clear.

The restaurant door was probably only ten feet

away now. I could make it. I had to.

As if to protest, Reef's wails became louder. I glanced back one more time.

If the man lunged at me, he could possibly reach me.

I glanced once more at Reef and gave it everything I had.

Directly in front of me, a man exited the restaurant. He saw me coming and held the door, a crease of concern forming between his eyebrows. I mumbled a quick "thank you" and darted into the restaurant.

I stopped right inside the door and drew in deep gulps of air, trying to even out my breathing.

When I looked around, everyone was staring at me. It was a bar, I realized. Not the normal place a woman with a baby frequented.

I pushed my hair behind my ear, not even caring at the moment that everyone around me had taken on judgmental expressions.

Glancing back, I saw the biker only feet away from the door. Would he come in here? Would he continue the confrontation in front of all these witnesses?

Someone that scary-looking might not care about the consequences. He might only care about the momentary gratification that came with keeping me quiet.

Thankfully, just then, a police cruiser pulled up out front.

I was safe.

Thank God, I was safe.

***

On the sidewalk right outside the bar as people gathered nearby and the sun started to disappear from sight, I gave Detective DePalma a rundown on what had happened on the sidewalk with Patrick.

Reef wailed the whole time. I took him from his stroller, noted that he'd messed his diaper again, and knew I was on borrowed time right now. The detective looked halfway annoyed that we couldn't talk without interruption, but what was I supposed to do?

Finally I excused myself, changed Reef in the bathroom of the bar, and then returned to the dark street. Numerous officers were still on the scene, the biker guys were still in the back of three police cars, and Patrick still looked totally freaked out as another detective talked to him only a few feet away.

His eyes were red and bloodshot. He continually ran his hands through his hair. Sweat sprinkled across his forehead and cheeks.

He was a man about to break.

I had to talk to him, but I had to use my time wisely if I wanted to do that. Inserting myself between him and the police would only be disastrous right now. At least Reef was content and quiet again.

Four months ago, I wouldn't have cared about what kind of impression I made or how best to handle the situation. I'd been brazen, outspoken, and headstrong, to name a few. Motherhood had not only changed my worldview, it had changed my body, my priorities, and my titles. In some unexplainable way, it had softened me and made me a little wiser.

Finally, just as Reef drifted to sleep in my arms, the police wrapped up their conversation with Patrick there on the sidewalk.

"Can I talk to him?" I asked the detective.

I had been waiting patiently for my turn, halfway fearful that Patrick would be arrested for illegal gambling and I wouldn't be able to speak with him at all. That didn't appear to be happening, though, so I had to grab my chance while I had the opportunity.

Detective DePalma stared at me like I'd lost my mind.

"Please. It's important."

Finally, he nodded. "If he'll talk to you, have at it." He turned away to look over his notes.

I approached Patrick, eyeing him carefully. He stood against the rough brick wall of the bar. He looked frazzled, like he hadn't slept in a week. His slight form appeared even more slight as he folded his arms over his chest.

Did he know who I was? Did he know about my connection with Mandee? I'd guess no.

Up close, I saw that Patrick's lip was busted and the area beneath his right eye was getting puffy. Those guys really had roughed him up. They would have done more if they'd had the opportunity.

"I guess I should say thank you," he mumbled,

uncrossing his arms and standing up straighter. "You distracted those guys before they could finish me off."

"Why are you in town?" I got right to the point. "I thought you were in Costa Rica."

He shifted and broke eye contact. "What do you mean?"

"I'm friends with Mandee. There's been quite a lot you've missed since you've been 'out of town.'"

Patrick cringed and let out a long sigh. "I was wondering if all of this would catch up with me."

"It has. You left your friend hanging out to dry, taking the fall for someone's death. Friends don't let friends go to jail for them." I paused dramatically. "Friends' lives matter."

His frown deepened as his shoulders slumped again. He sagged against the wall behind him. "None of this was supposed to happen. I was going to come forward and admit that I was in town. I just had to get this mess straightened out first. I had to disappear."

"What mess would that be?"

He ran a hand over his face. "I got into some financial trouble."

"How?" I pressed.

"I took up gambling on the side and made some bad bets."

Gambling? Gambling was somehow tied in with this? I hadn't seen that one coming. "Why in the world did you take up gambling? Especially with those guys."

"I need money."

"And as soon as you graduate and get a job in engineering, you'll have it." People who tried to take the easy way out always annoyed me. Like, really annoyed me. I didn't have much, but I'd fought for everything I had and even refused the help of my parents in order to make my own way.

"I don't want a job in engineering."

"But that's what you're studying."

"How'd you know that?" A wrinkle formed between his eyes, and he looked at me like I was a mind reader or something.

"I have a way of finding out these things."

He grunted. "Okay then. My parents want me to have a secure job that I can fall back on."

"Oh." That made sense. Parental pressure was a real thing. I understood that. My parents wanted me to go into medicine, but I'd refused. Then again, as Chad said, I was one of the most stubborn people ever.

"I want to be a photographer, but it's hard to jump right into that career and make enough money to support yourself. It's all I've ever wanted to do, though. I figured if I just had a little money to get me by, maybe I could truly make a go at it."

"But . . . ?" I knew there was more to this story.

"I was doing well, so I got into this gambling circle. I actually made around twenty thousand in my first month. But I got cocky. I thought I was on a roll. I lost it all, and now I owe big time."

"When you realized you had to pay up, you ran?"

He nodded. "Exactly. I knew I had to disappear. But I couldn't leave all of my animals to fend for themselves. It wasn't the right thing to do. So I asked Mandee to stay at my house, and I started staying at the shelter at night."

"At least *that* was noble of you." I narrowed my eyes. "Somehow these guys found you."

He nodded. "I'm not sure how it happened, but they were pretty determined."

I leveled my gaze with him. "Did you kill Tag Wilson?"

He blinked. "What? . . . No."

"You do realize he's dead, don't you?"

He ran a hand through his hair again. "Yeah. I do realize that. I heard."

"Yet you still didn't come out of the woodwork?"

"My own life was on the line. Those guys would have killed me."

"What happened to that vent?"

"I have no idea. I didn't do it. I didn't want Tag dead."

I wasn't dropping this that easily. "I heard that the two of you didn't get along."

"We didn't. But I wouldn't have killed him. Or even tried to scare him. I promise. All I want to do is take pictures. Ask anyone who knows me, and they'll tell you."

"Any idea who might have wanted to kill Tag?"

He nodded without hesitation. "Jim Benson from Jungle Jim's. He's the one who did this."

CHAPTER 13

"Why in the world would you think that?" I asked, rocking Reef back and forth in the stroller to keep him quiet.

He shifted and glanced back at Detective DePaula, who listened from a few feet away and had begun to impatiently tap his foot. I couldn't blame him. This conversation was taking longer than I'd anticipated. Not only that, but a small crowd had formed to check out what was going on. The three guys who'd tried to jump Patrick were shooting death glares at Patrick. It had also grown dark outside, which made everything feel creepier.

"Jim bought Chalice from this guy in North Carolina. The snake had been the guy's uncle's. His uncle died, and this guy just wanted to purge the house of all his things, so he sold everything for super cheap"

"Okay . . ." I wasn't sure where he was going with this.

"Jim doesn't consider himself a snake expert, by any stretch of the imagination. In fact, in case you ever noticed, he doesn't actually sell any snakes in his pet store.

He ended up keeping Chalice at home and began asking around about anyone who wanted to buy it."

"Okay."

"Tag told Jim about me. Jim contacted me, and I bought Chalice. She was beautiful and unique, and I paid nearly three hundred dollars for her—more money than I should have spent, but I couldn't resist."

"You didn't know Jim before this, correct?"

He nodded. "That's right. Tag had connected us. Before that, I'd bought most of my animals online. I don't love pet stores, so I try to avoid them. But I couldn't resist Chalice. She was beautiful."

"How does that mean Jim is guilty? Just because he sold you the snake?" So far, this conversation was getting me nowhere.

"Jim wanted Chalice back. I don't know what changed. He seemed perfectly content to sell her to me. But, about a month later, he started calling me, making up all these excuses about why an apartment was no place for Chalice."

"Why'd he change his mind?"

Patrick frowned. "Out of the blue, Tag was uncomfortable with the snake. That could have been part of it."

"But you think there's more to it?"

He nodded. "Yeah, of course. I mean, Tag was the one who connected us, and suddenly he did a one-eighty? What sense does that make?"

I had to agree. It seemed weird. Too bad Tag

wasn't around anymore to explain himself. Something was fishy.

"Any theories as to why?"

He shook his head. "I have no idea. But something else was going on. Tag went as far as to report me to Animal Control for a violation."

"He actually did that?" I'd thought it had only been an idle threat.

Patrick nodded. "Yeah, I got a notice right before I went into hiding."

But there was something that still didn't fit . . ."What about the one thousand dollars the two of you were talking about at The Grounds a few days ago?"

Patrick's face went pale, and I knew I'd caught him in some kind of untruth. "I don't know what you're talking about."

I wasn't letting him off the hook that easily. "Someone overheard the two of you discussing it."

He stiffened. "Well, they heard wrong."

"Time's up, Ms. Davis. We've got to wrap this up," the detective said.

"What about Mandee? Why did you involve her in all this?" I rushed.

"I knew she loved animals," he finally said.

"You knew she was naïve," I countered.

He looked away again, and I knew I'd hit on the truth. He'd used Mandee, knowing no one else would want to take care of his snakes. No one else would have stayed around through all the drama.

And now she was in jail because of it.

The detective took over and began questioning Patrick again.

As I left, I felt in one way that I had some answers. But those answers just led to more questions. I needed a few more minutes to question Patrick. I couldn't let this drop.

I needed to talk to Patrick again sometime. I hoped it wasn't as hard—or dangerous—to track him down the second time around.

***

I went to church with Gabby the next morning, and we grabbed lunch together at a local Mexican restaurant known for its canned mariachi music and the cheerful paper lantern hanging from the ceiling.

Riley and Gabby sat in the booth across from me, and Reef was tucked in his car seat beside me, staring at a colorful toy strapped across the handles.

As soon as the chips and salsa were delivered, the conversation had turned to Mandee.

"Mandee is a very interesting girl," Riley said, popping a chip in his mouth. As soon as he swallowed, he picked up another chip and stared at it. "I knew we shouldn't have come to this restaurant. These chips are irresistible."

"Just pretend they're full of protein instead of processed corn and fat," Gabby told him.

Riley raised his eyebrows. "Yeah, I'll do my best."

"Apparently you made quite the impression on Mandee," I told Riley.

It was Gabby's turn to raise her eyebrows. "Did you?"

He raised his palms in innocence. "I'm sure it was my legal skills that impressed her."

"Yeah, I'm sure." Gabby flashed a knowing smile.

These two were so in love. I wished they'd go ahead and get married. I wasn't sure why Gabby seemed to keep coming up with excuses to delay. I'd tried to talk to her about it, but she never had much to say. She seemed to just be enjoying the moment.

"What do you think will happen to her?" I asked Riley, taking a sip of my lemon water.

"It's hard to say. If you put all the evidence together, it doesn't look good. Especially the crowbar and the fight and the Facebook threats. I don't think a jury will be compelled to convict her, but I've seen some crazy trials lately. One of the other lawyers at my firm was representing a family where the guy shot a burglar who broke into their home. The burglar won. None of us could believe it."

Reef cooed beside me, and my heart did flips. I wanted to treasure these moments.

"That's crazy," I muttered.

A man sitting in the booth on the other side of the room raised a newspaper, and I squirmed when I saw it. The second part of Chloe's editorial should be in there. I really had to figure out how I was going to handle that whole situation. It was just one more thing on my plate.

Why couldn't we be getting attention for our crusades against animal testing? Or against fast food chains that used barbaric practices to slaughter animals? Or the fur industry, which had no redeeming qualities whatsoever?

Instead, we were getting attention for Chalice.

"What's wrong?" Gabby's eyebrows knitted together.

I explained my dilemma.

"I guess this is one of the downsides to being the boss, huh? The buck stops with you," Gabby said. "What do you think about Chalice?"

That was the question of the hour. Of the day. Of the week, for that matter. "A year ago I would have welcomed any attention I could get for our causes. But now I just keep thinking: What if it had been Reef? What if my son had been the victim? Then would I still want this snake out there?"

At that moment, our food was delivered. A bean burrito for me, chicken fajitas without tortillas for Riley, and a beef chimichanga for Gabby. The sizzling scent of grilled peppers and onions wafted toward me, and my stomach growled.

Reef let out a loud cry of joy beside me. I looked over and saw him staring at my food. He looked like he was hungry also. In the blink of an eye, I would be ordering tacos for him. He'd be seated beside me in a little booster, and eventually he'd want to feed himself. The days were going by so quickly already. I wished time would slow down.

"You mind if I pray before we eat?" Riley said.

"Not at all."

I closed my eyes as Riley offered thanks for the food, and then we all dug in. The conversation picked up right where we'd left off.

"Being a mom has a tendency to soften people and smooth out rough edges," Gabby said. "That's what I've heard, at least."

"I just keep thinking: What if Chalice goes to another home and does this again? What if I had a role in this? If I had a role in keeping her alive? That would make the blame partly ours. Partly *mine*."

"The fault wouldn't lie with you, but I can understand the pressure you're feeling," Riley said. "It's people's lives that are on the line."

"Which is so weird because I'm usually so focused on animal lives." *Animal Lives Matter.*

The slogan was brilliant. Catchy. Chalice made a good poster animal for the crusade, I supposed. But something in my gut just couldn't go along with all of this. It was like I told Patrick last night: Friends' Lives Matter. People's Lives Matter. Everyone got one chance at this thing called life, and we all deserved a fair shot.

"So what are you going to do?" Riley asked before taking a bite of his lunch.

"I still don't know. If I pull the plug on this, I look

like a bad leader. Truth is I *have* been a bad leader lately. I've been distracted, and I don't feel like I'm doing anything well: not being a wife or a mother or the director of a well-known animal rights group." Tears popped to my eyes.

Tears? Where had they come from? I wasn't a crier.

"Cut yourself some slack." Gabby patted my hand. "With time, things will start feeling normal again."

"You speak as if you know."

She shrugged. "I have no idea. I'm not a mom, of course." She glanced at Riley, and I could see it in her eyes that she wanted to have kids one day. "But I know life can throw curveballs. We have to redefine our normal. We have to adjust in order to survive."

Yes, Gabby did understand all of that. Her life had certainly been turned upside down enough times.

Gratitude filled me that I had understanding friends in my life. I'd thought for the longest time that all I'd needed was my cats. I'd been wrong.

"Thanks for the talk, guys," I told them. "What would I do without you?"

***

After we ate, I ran to the grocery store with Reef. Loaded with some fresh fruits and veggies, at least I had that worry behind me. Then, back at home, I sat at the little desk tucked away in the corner of my bedroom to pay bills while Reef sat in his favorite bouncy seat, looking content to stare at the toys on the front of it and listen to "Mary Had a Little Lamb."

If I finished in time, Gabby and I had talked about going to the park for a walk. It was beautiful outside—not too hot and not too cold. Having some time alone with Gabby would be nice, so I hoped it worked out.

If that didn't work out, then I would probably end up calling back some of the reporters who had left me messages this weekend about the campaign to save Chalice. I'd been putting it off, which was unlike me. I wasn't usually the wishy-washy type. But I needed to think this through and come up with a solution I could live with.

As I wrote a check for my car payment, an idea hit me. I called one of my employees to pick her brain about something.

"Julia, sorry to bother you on a Sunday." Julia was a sweet employee who was on the younger side and who'd only been with us a few months. But I seemed to remember one of our first conversations, and I needed to ask her about it.

"It's no problem. What's up?"

"You used to work at Jungle Jim's, didn't you?" If I remembered correctly, it was her time at that pet shop that had made her decide to come work for Animal Protective Services. She couldn't stand to see how some of the animals were treated.

Silence hung on the line for a moment. "That's right. I hate that place. If I could find a way to close it down, I'd do it."

"I hear you. Listen, the owner, Jim Benson. What do you know about him?"

"Jim Benson? He's a horrible man who puts profits above anything else. He's despicable, as far as I'm concerned. He belongs right up here with Hitler."

At one time, I might have agreed with her assessments. I still felt like he was a horrible man. But Hitler? I wouldn't take it that far.

"And he has monkey lips."

Ah ha! Someone else thought so too. Hearing it voiced out loud didn't sound very nice, though.

"Listen, Julia," I started. "Jim sold an albino python to someone, and later said he had second thoughts about the safety of his decision. How does that hit you?"

"Like I said, if Jim makes money, that's all he cares about. Safety has never been a top priority for him. For him to go out of his way to say he's concerned? That sounds fishy to me."

I nodded. "I've met Jim several times, and I was thinking the same thing. This guy with the snake—he said Jim even went as far as to offer to buy this python back. Jim is acting like he was being a good citizen and doing this for the betterment of community."

"I doubt it. That doesn't sound like the Jim I know." She paused. "Speaking of which, is this the same python that's been on the news?"

I remembered that whole campaign and let out a mental sigh. "It is."

"The media really picked up that story and ran with it, didn't they?"

"Yes, they did."

"You never know what's going to stick. I guess that's why you throw a lot of stuff against the wall, right?"

"In a way. But, on the other hand, we need to be purposeful. But that's not what I wanted to talk to you about." I tapped my fingers together, trying to think all of this through. "Do you know anyone who works at Jungle Jim's still?"

"I do have a couple of friends there. Why?"

"Would you mind doing some digging for me?"

Her voice rang with delight. "I'd love to. In fact, I'll do that right now."

CHAPTER 14

An hour later, Julia had some answers. And she became my new favorite employee.

"I talked to two people who worked there. One was clueless. But the other guy—I think he used to like me—was more than willing to spill the beans. He just so happened to overhear a conversation between Jim and a man he'd never seen before. I think it might fit with what you were asking me about earlier."

I leaned back at my desk, where I was still paying bills, balancing my checkbook, and calculating how far Chad and I were in our quest to save money for a down payment on a house. Easy answer: not very far. It was going to be a long time before we got there.

I turned back to my phone conversation with Julia. "When did this conversation between Jim and another man occur?"

"About a week ago."

"Very interesting." It fit the timetable for when things started going south with Patrick and his snake.

"What was said?"

"This other guy was from New York, and apparently he 'collects' exotic animals. He wants an albino python, and he'd heard that Jim had one."

My first thought was: collects exotic animals? What a monster. People were supposed to collect spoons or dolls or even cars. Not animals that they had no intention of loving and caring for.

My second thought was: someone who was obsessed with albino pythons might go to great lengths to get what they wanted. I'd seen it happen many times before. In reality, I had gone to great lengths to get what I wanted. Usually it involved animals and their protection.

Like this case right now. Even though I had a million things to do, I couldn't drop this. It was more than about Mandee being accused of a crime.

This whole predicament was a travesty for Chalice, for Mandee, and for Tag.

"So this guy wanted Chalice for himself, huh?" I said.

"Yes, he did. In fact, this guy was willing to pay top dollar."

I glanced at the number at the bottom of my checkbook. The only thing I could pay top dollar for right now was organic food, and even that was a stretch. "Did your friend define 'top dollar'?"

"About twenty grand."

"For a snake?" My mouth dropped open, and I forgot about my own checkbook. Who in their right mind would pay that much for a snake?

"This guy is determined to get one."

I stared out the window at the house behind mine, trying to sort through my thoughts. "So what if Jim wanted to buy Chalice back, not for safety reasons, but so he could make a killer profit?"

"It's a possibility. A very real one."

I chewed on my bottom lip a moment in thought. "There's only one thing that doesn't make sense. Chalice is now in the custody of Animal Control. So if Jim was behind all of this, his plan majorly backfired."

"You can say that again."

I tapped my pen on the desk in thought. "I still think there could be something there."

"What are you going to do?"

I glanced at my watch. "I'm going to swing by Jungle Jim's and have a little heart-to-heart."

***

Jim's hand was buried deep in a hamster cage when I spotted him in the store. He grunted when he saw me, and I hoped he wasn't squeezing an innocent hamster in retaliation for my presence.

"You again," he muttered.

"I have some questions," I told him, coming to a stop beside the cage. Reef's eyes brightened as he looked around the store at the colorful images of animals that had been painted on the cement walls.

Jim continued to try and grab a hamster that was desperate to get away from him. Even rodents seemed to know Jim was trouble.

"I'm sure you do," he said. "I'm not interested in talking to you."

I took note of several customers within hearing distance and raised my voice. "I'd be more than happy to talk right here about how your actions may have led to the murder of one of your customer's neighbors."

Several people nearby stopped and gawked. I sent Jim a satisfied smirk because that was just the reaction I'd hoped for.

"Fine." He pulled his hand from the cage and gave the hamster a dirty look. "Let's talk in my office."

I didn't necessarily want to be alone with the man, but several witnesses had seen me here. If anything happened to me, Jim would be the first person the police looked at.

I hoped.

Jim's office was small, and it smelled like a litter box that hadn't been cleaned in days. It was a wonder he was able to work in here with all of the clutter and inventory being stored in the space. Despite that, Jim cleared a chair and motioned for me to sit. Then he went to the other side of the desk, removed several stacks of paper that acted as a blockade, and then sat down in a battered chair.

Before the conversation started, something in the corner of the room caught my eye. It was a pole with a rope on the end. The kind people used when handling snakes or other animals. Interesting. Did Jim really need one of these here? He mostly carried small animals and puppies.

"What in the world are you talking about?" Jim roared when we were out of sight. "I knew you were crazy, but I had no idea you were that crazy."

If he thought he was insulting me, he was wrong. I was okay with being called crazy. In fact, I'd been called much, much worse. I did have the impulse to cover Reef's ears, however. He shouldn't have to hear his mother being talked to like this.

"You sold Patrick that snake, and then you wanted it back because you got a higher bidder." I put it all out there and watched his reaction.

He pulled his face back, the action creating multiple chins. But he wasn't fooling me. His surprise was staged. He had to have known all this was coming.

"I don't know what you're talking about," he said, his voice devoid of emotion.

I locked him in place with my gaze. "I think you do. What I'm trying to figure out is why you'd kill to get what you wanted."

He raised his hands in the air, his emotions suddenly springing to life. "I didn't kill no one."

I leaned closer. "Let's face it: Patrick wasn't willing to sell you back that snake. He loved Chalice too much. That's why you took matters into your own hands."

"Don't be ridiculous. Besides, why would I murder

Tag to get Chalice?"

That was an excellent question. I had no idea. But I wasn't dropping this. "I think what you really wanted was for Chalice to escape to Tag's apartment. Maybe you never meant for things to go so terribly wrong. You never thought your friend would be murdered. Instead, you thought you'd get the snake and sell it to this guy for a nice profit."

One of his eyebrows twitched up as a thoughtful expression captured his face. "It's not a bad idea. But I didn't do it. Do you know how hard it would be to steal a snake that weighs as much as Chalice? It would be impossible. I couldn't exactly sneak Chalice into my coat and be on my way."

"But if the snake was in Tag's apartment, it would be much easier."

He shrugged stiffly. "Maybe. But I didn't do it."

"You did want the snake back, didn't you? Can you at least own up to that?"

He let out a long sigh. "Fine. I did offer to buy it back. I'd found a buyer willing to pay top dollar for a snake like Chalice, so I tried to buy the snake back from Patrick. I told him the snake was too dangerous to have in an apartment building like that. But Patrick wasn't falling for it. He wanted Chalice all for himself."

Well, that was one answer, but I still had more questions. "So you're telling me you know nothing about how Chalice got into your friend's apartment?"

He maintained eye contact with me. "That's exactly

what I'm telling you."

"Do you have an alibi for the evening Tag died?"

He sat back and nodded, a satisfied expression on his face. "As a matter of fact, I do. One of the dogs here hurt his leg right before closing. I was here with the vet all night. I'll give you his number."

CHAPTER 15

As I stepped out of Jungle Jim's, I called Patrick. He couldn't hide behind the excuse that he was out of the country and without cell service any more.

That said, I was surprised when he actually answered.

"It's Sierra," I said.

"Who?"

"We met yesterday. I'm Mandee's friend. I saved you before the Vikings could tear your head off."

"Oh yeah. Right. Thanks again for that."

"We need to talk," I said, trying to put Reef into the car without dropping the phone.

"That can't happen. I have to remain out of sight. There are still Vikings out there who'd love nothing more than to beat me to a pulp."

"It's of vital importance, Patrick. Do you really want Mandee to go the prison for something you did?"

"Of course not."

"Then meet me."

"How do I know you're not being followed?"

"You don't."

"I'll meet you at The Grounds in ten minutes. Make sure no one is tailing you, though. My life depends on it."

I really had no idea if anyone was tailing me or not, but I did glance in the rearview mirror several times on my way through downtown Norfolk. Best I could tell, I was okay. Besides, wouldn't a member of the Vikings be on a motorcycle? Certainly I would spot them then.

When I walked into The Grounds, I didn't see Patrick. I saw college kids and some young adults and an older couple with an elementary-aged grandson. I saw Sharon, Clarice, and a homeless guy in the corner.

No Patrick.

I frowned.

"Can I hold Reef?" Clarice asked, rushing over.

I nodded and helped Clarice get him out of the car seat. She took him over to the pastries to show him what he had to look forward to one day when he could chew.

While she did that, I scanned the crowds one more time. My gaze stopped on the homeless man. He looked up at me, and that's when the first spark of recognition hit me.

It was Patrick.

What?

"Can you watch Reef for a minute, Clarice?" I asked.

She nodded. "Take as much time as you want."

I hurried across the coffee shop and slid into the

chair across from him. Though he was dressed like a homeless man, a close inspection belied his true state. His clothes were old, but the tears were purposeful. He didn't even smell like someone who lived on the streets.

"Patrick?"

He shrugged. "This is my disguise for now. I have nowhere else to go."

"Really? Nowhere at all? Your parents' house maybe?"

"Wherever I go, people will be in danger. So I'm dressing like this and staying on the streets for a while. It's actually been very enlightening."

I didn't have time to converse with him about it now. I had other questions for him. "I need you to tell me what's really going on."

"I already did."

"I need you to tell me everything. There's something you're leaving out."

"I don't know what you're talking about," he insisted.

"Please, Patrick. I'm only trying to help Mandee. I know that Tag told you his friend Jim had a python he'd just gotten in that he was trying to sell. You bought Chalice for less than three hundred dollars. But then, for some reason, Tag flipped. He was suddenly afraid of the snake and wanted you to sell it back to Jim. Why is that?"

Patrick frowned and stared at the tabletop a moment. "There is more to the story," he finally said.

"Please tell me what. I need to know, Patrick."

"The first part of the story is true. Tag and I got along just fine at the beginning. And that whole thing about hating snakes—it was partially true—but as long as I kept the snakes to myself, Tag was fine with them."

"But something changed," I prodded.

He nodded. "That's right. Jim came to me and wanted to buy Chalice back. He said she was a safety risk. That the snake was too big to be kept in a residential apartment complex. Tag got in on it also and even threatened to call Animal Control. It was weird."

"What happened next?"

"Jim kept pressing, and I kept saying no. He even offered one thousand dollars to me at one point, which I thought was suspicious. I mean, it seemed over the top and not like the Jim I first met."

"I agree. He offered you almost three times what you paid. It was enough to raise red flags for anyone."

Patrick nodded. "Exactly!"

Before he could finish, Sharon placed some coffee in front of Patrick. "Another customer wanted you to have this," she said.

The grandparents across the room waved to him. Patrick waved back. "People really can be kind. It almost makes me want to turn my focus from photographing animals to people. But that's not what you want to talk to me about."

"No, please continue." Although, I had to admit the subject was interesting to me because I understood the pull between pouring everything into people or pouring it into animals.

"Finally, one day Tag came to me. He told me that Jim had confided in him that someone offered to buy Chalice for a hefty price tag. He was talking thousands of dollars."

"Twenty thousand?"

Patrick's eyes widened. "How'd you know? Actually, never mind. Anyway, Tag said he would find out the name of this buyer for me if I would split part of the profit. He wanted 40 percent."

"That's quite the commission."

Patrick nodded. "It is. But then I started thinking about it. As much as I love Chalice, I could really use that money. I could pay my gambling debt and start my photography business. It would have really gone a long way."

"I can see that."

"Then I realized that I really shouldn't have to pay Tag that much. I did some research and found the name of this guy myself. I emailed him about buying Chalice."

"Did Tag find out?"

Patrick grimaced. "He did. And he wasn't happy. He wasn't happy at all. That's when he started causing a ruckus. He told everyone in the apartment building how dangerous Chalice was. He called Animal Control on me, and they sent me a warning. I think Jim and Tag thought that as soon as I got a warning, I would automatically want to sell Chalice back to Jim. But I didn't. Tag was mad."

"Whatever happened to this buyer?"

"The timing was awful. He had to take a business trip to India, and it was right when I needed the money. He's supposed to get back on Wednesday. Of course, now they're talking about putting Chalice down, so any hope I have of selling her went down the toilet."

"Tag did threaten to ruin your plan, Patrick. Killing him would ensure the money remained all yours."

Patrick shook his head. "But killing him with Chalice would only ensure my snake ended up on death row. It would have been a bad plan."

I frowned, unable to argue. "You're right."

He picked up his disposable coffee cup and nodded. "I've got to run now before I'm spotted."

"Thanks for meeting with me."

He took a step away but paused. "One more thing."

"What's that?" I hoped it was something useful.

"Would you feed my geckos for me?"

***

I'd been hoping that Mandee might try to call me again because I had a question for her.

That evening, she did. She seemed intent on using her one phone call a day to call me. I didn't even want to think about how much all these collect calls were costing.

I just happened to be at Patrick's apartment feeding his geckos and frogs again when she phoned.

Gabby had agreed to postpone our walk and had come with me to Patrick's place. She stayed in the living room with Reef as I dropped some crickets into the tank.

I shoved my cell phone between my shoulder and ear. "Mandee, I need you to think carefully. Did anyone stop by while you were at Patrick's taking care of his animals?"

"They're not really *his* animals. I mean, he doesn't *own* them because you can't *own* animals—"

"Mandee, I need you to focus." Irritation pinched my spine, but I had to admit—she'd caught me. I needed to watch my wording. I was slipping lately. "Did anyone stop by Patrick's apartment?"

She paused a moment. "Not really. I mean, I guess there were those motorcycle guys."

The irritation pinched harder at my spine as I closed the lid to the gecko's enclosure. "Motorcycle guys stopped by?"

"I didn't mention that?"

"No, you didn't." Mandee had an amazing knack for forgetting important details.

"Oh, well, they did. They were looking for Patrick, but I told them he was out of town."

"How did they handle that news?"

She paused a moment. "Okay, I guess. I mean, they mostly grunted. I think they said they would come back later or something."

"I see. Anyone else you can think of?" I waved at the little corn snake who still swayed his body against the glass like he needed some attention. Poor thing.

"Hmm . . . the landlord stopped by once. He

seemed like a nice guy."

It took a moment for her words to settle into my thoughts that something was wrong with her statement. "The landlord is a woman."

"No, *he's* not," she said it in a singsong voice that made me want to reach through the phone line and give her a wet willie.

"I met her. She's a woman. In her sixties." I clearly remembered the encounter when I'd told her I'd be checking out Patrick's apartment.

"Don't be ridiculous. He's a man. In his early forties maybe? He had a big, bushy mustache just like my Uncle Will used to have."

Big, bushy mustache? I'd only met one person recently with a mustache like that.

Brian Bunch.

It looked like I needed to pay him another visit.

CHAPTER 16

"Sierra, check this out," Gabby said when I stepped out of the reptile room.

She was kneeling on the floor, which was wooden and painted a dark red color.

"What is it?" I didn't see anything, even when I stooped closer. I expected to see a hair or some other kind of trace evidence that someone like Gabby was trained to look for. All I saw was the wooden planks, the ugly paint job, and a bit of dirt.

"Look at these indentations." She pointed at something. "Do you see them?"

I looked more closely, squinting to see beyond the shadows being cast by the dim overhead light. "Yeah, I guess I do see them, now that you mention it."

They were about the size of a nickel, and I could see the mark every foot or so. They seemed to lead from the front door all the way to the hallway where the bedrooms were.

"I don't see how these marks are relevant," I

CHRISTY BARRITT

finished.

Gabby twisted her lips in thought and stood. "I don't know either. But I think they're new. The wood still looks fresh where the indentions were made. The wood these floors are made of is soft so anything could have done this."

"Like what?"

She drew in a long breath. "Well, high heels—except they're too far apart to be high heels."

"I concur."

"Chair legs?" she continued.

"The spacing is odd for chair legs."

Gabby's eyes lit. "What about one of those snake hooks?"

"A snake hook?" Realization swarmed through me. "Jim had one in his office."

"Could he have come here to try and steal the snake, only things went wrong?"

"It's something to think about."

Gabby stood and leaned against the wall, staring off in the distance in thought. "But there's one other thing I can't figure out. It's the fact that this Brian Bunch guy showed up at Patrick's door pretending to be the landlord. Why would he do that? Does it tie in with the death of Tag Wilson?"

"I have no idea. Maybe he was secretly seeing if anyone was at home. If Mandee hadn't answered, maybe he would have tried to get inside himself."

"To get to the snake?"

I shrugged. "I'm not even sure he knew about the snake. However, Mandee said when she made the idle threat against Tag that she posted it on Facebook. She could have even tagged his name on there, for all I know. If she did, any of Tag's enemies who saw his page would have known that someone with a snake was angry at him."

Gabby looked uncertain, but I could tell her mind was processing everything and formulating ideas and theories. "He could have done that, but he would need a strong motive. I mean, he knew Tag, not Patrick, right?"

I nodded. "As far as I know, the two of them didn't know each other."

"I'm not saying Brian doesn't have some kind of reason for coming to Patrick's. But we're just taking stabs at things at this point."

"I agree. I have only guesses."

She started pacing. She'd been doing that lately when she was thinking things through. "He would also have to know that Patrick had snakes, that he lived above Tag, and he would be operating on the hope that the snake would actually drop into the vent and into the neighbor's apartment. There are a lot of probabilities there. If someone really wanted to kill this guy, this wasn't the best plan, except for the fact that it would be difficult not to get caught."

"How would we even begin to find out what his motive might be?" I sighed and plopped down onto Patrick's couch.

"The only way to do that would be to talk to people

who know Brian," Gabby said. "You could check his social media account. His friends should be listed. It's surprising how many times you may have mutual friends or recognize people there. It would be a good place to start."

I stood. "Let's do it."

Her eyebrows shot up. "You're going to use Patrick's computer?"

"Why not?" I sat at his desk, which was still cleared from the last time I was here. I turned on his computer. Just as I hoped, he didn't have it password protected. I opened the Internet and typed in Brian Bunch's name.

The first results that popped up were mostly his business: Bunch Systems. But as I scrolled farther, his name came up attached to a video on a social media site. Out of curiosity, I clicked on it.

My eyes widened as I realized what I was watching.

Gabby appeared behind me. "What are you doing?"

"Um . . . it said Brian Bunch, so I clicked on it."

It was some kind of recording, probably taken on a cell phone camera. In the background, there were various people milling around . . . except I wasn't sure they were people. They almost looked like . . . superheroes?

"This is weird," Gabby muttered, leaning closer.

"Tell me about it." I continued to watch, more curious than ever, about where this video was going.

The video continued to record a group of costumed adults. Yes, these were definitely people who were dressed up as superheroes. They wore all kinds of crazy outfits with capes and leotards and masks. It could have been shot at some kind of convention, based on the comic book signs in the background. Could this get weirder?

The man taking the video laughed, at first lightly, but harder and harder as he zoomed in on one person. It was a man wearing a gold cape, red tights, and a blue onesie. I gasped when I saw his bushy mustache.

"I can't believe this," the man recording the video whispered. "There he is. Brian Bunch, Mr. Tough Ex-Military Security Expert. What does he do in his free time? He dresses like a superhero. A superhero!" The man cackled.

A bit of a green leaf appeared at the edge of the screen. Someone was recording this while hiding. Tag. It had to be Tag.

"I think you found your motive," Gabby said. "Putting something like this online would put Brian's reputation in jeopardy, which fits after Tag was fired. It would be humiliating. It could make someone mad enough . . . to murder."

"I need to talk to Brian."

"How are you going to track him down tonight?"

I hit a few more keys until I found his social media profile. Thankfully, Brian was the type of person who liked to announce to the world where he was going. It wasn't very smart for someone who prided himself in being a security expert. But it worked to my advantage right now.

I pointed to the screen at the words "Holden's Gym" before looking at Gabby. "I'm going to work out. You want to come?"

A huge grin spread across her face. "You know it."
Reef cooed in agreement.

***

"Do you think I look out of place being here with Reef?" I
asked.

"Like a beach house in Colorado," Gabby muttered,
glancing around the gym. "But you know what they say?
Go big or go home."

She started singing a song by the same name,
holding an imaginary microphone and raising her other
hand in the air like she was in concert. Her mini show only
lasted about ten seconds before she got serious again. It
was classic Gabby.

I looked around. This wasn't one of those family-
friendly gyms with a childcare area and a smoothie bar.
No, this was a small gym full of bodybuilders, sweat, and
lots of grunting.

Gabby and I stood out like . . . well, beach houses in
Colorado. Gabby wore her jeans, T-shirt, and flip-flops. I
wore khakis, and a black T-shirt with loafers. Nothing
about us screamed, "I want to work out!"

"Can I help you?" a sculpted woman at the front
desk asked.

Just as she asked the question, I spotted Brian
Bunch walking toward the exit with a towel draped over
his shoulders.

Perfect!

"No, we're good," I told the woman, quickly doing a U-turn and falling in step beside Brian. "Fancy seeing you here."

He paused and stared at me a moment as Gabby came up on his other side. He visibly bristled.

"You came into my office Friday," he finally said, looking tense and as if he expected a confrontation.

I nodded and pushed my glasses up higher on my nose. "I did."

"What are you doing here? I can only assume you're not working out. Not wearing that and with a baby strapped to your chest."

"Well, carrying him is quite the workout, but you're right. I'm here to talk to you."

He paused by the door, which was good. I wanted to talk to him in public where there would be plenty of witnesses.

"About what?" he asked, his gaze still suspicious.

"Tag Wilson, of course."

Something flickered in his eyes. "I already answered your questions."

"We have more," Gabby added.

Brian twisted his head ever-so-slightly as he turned to look at Gabby. "Who are you?"

"She's one of the area's top forensic experts," I answered. It was a slight exaggeration. Actually, Gabby was brilliant. Some people were just slow to recognize that.

"Forensic expert?" He squinted, partly with alarm. "I'm still not sure what you both are doing here."

Gabby nodded at me. This was usually her territory, but she was giving me the lead here to launch my questions.

"We know you went to Patrick Roper's apartment a couple of days before your former employee Tag Wilson died," I said.

He shrugged, his gaze scanning the gym behind me.

He was uncomfortable and cornered. Good. I didn't want him to be too relaxed.

"So what if I did? Is that illegal?" His arms went to his hips.

"How exactly did you know Patrick?" Gabby asked.

"I didn't. I'd only heard about him. Tag had started talking about those stupid snakes nonstop in the days before I fired him. Mr. Tough Guy didn't want to admit it, but he hated snakes. That was why he wanted his neighbor to get rid of them."

"What's that have to do with you visiting Patrick?" I asked, still not connecting the dots.

He sighed and looked to the side again. He was contemplating whether or not to tell us the truth or a lie. He had the classic body language for it. I hoped he chose wisely because I was going to find out either way.

His jaw flexed but he said nothing.

Maybe he just needed some more prodding. "I know about the video Tag posted of you wearing the . . . well, you know." I glanced around, trying to make it clear that I'd announce his secret to anyone close enough to hear.

Brian's cheeks turned red. "My lawyer drew up a cease and desist letter for Tag. He had no business posting that video for all the world to see, nor did he have any grounds for following me. That's called stalking."

"Why did he do it? Did he hate you that much?"

His jaw flexed. "He threatened to post it if I didn't rescind the termination of his job and reinstate him."

"A type of blackmail, huh? Tag wasn't a very nice person, was he?"

Brian scowled, becoming tenser by the moment. "You could say that."

"Apparently you stood strong and didn't rehire him," I said, prodding for more information.

"That's right. I can't let bullies get what they want. I gave him plenty of warnings concerning his job, and he made no effort to change. He's typical of today's society— he wants to blame everyone else for his own failings."

"It sounds like he must have been very bitter," I said.

"To say the least. He said he had bills to pay. I get that. I do."

"He could have just gotten another job," Gabby said.

"Exactly! It's a free market. Only I had a non-compete disclosure in his contract." Something close to satisfaction stained his gaze, like he enjoyed having the upper hand.

"Why?" Gabby asked. "Do you have proof of concept ideas or something? That kind of clause is usually reserved for innovative types of businesses."

"We do a few things that are highly specialized. If my competitors were to learn our exact methods, my business could be compromised."

"So he couldn't have simply gotten another job. It sounds more complicated than that." I thought about that as two body builders pushed their way past. "You're a tough guy. It's like you said: you didn't want that video out there."

He tugged at the collar of his muscle shirt, which was already plenty loose. "Look, I know it's weird. I know what people think. But it's nice sometimes just to feel anonymous, and that's what those costumes allow. As strange as it may seem, it's my release from the stress of managing my business."

"That still doesn't explain why you went to Patrick's apartment," I countered, trying still to get to that prized pearl at the center of this.

He shrugged stiffly. "I just wanted to teach him a lesson."

"By scaring him with a snake?" Gabby countered.

"It wasn't like that. I just wanted to prank him. Catch it on video. Have something to hold as leverage over him. I thought Tag's neighbor might want to get in on it with me. It's hard enough to get a date, without a video like that out there." He squirmed and ran a hand through his thick hair.

"Did your prank turn into murder?" I asked.

His gaze scanned everyone around us, and he let out a nervous laugh. "Of course not! I learned that Patrick wasn't home so I backed off. It was a decision I contemplated in the heat of the moment. I knew Tag was gone all day, working the fields at a farm in Virginia Beach for some extra cash, so I stopped by. As soon as I learned that Patrick was out of town, I forgot about it."

Ah ha! That's why Tag had manure on his boots. "Can you prove that you weren't involved?"

He pressed his lips together before letting out a long sigh. "That night I had another meeting with my . . . superhero friends. They can verify I was there all night. I'll give you their phone numbers. Just please—don't let this leak. My business—not to mention my reputation—would be ruined."

"I'll take those phone numbers," I said, reserving my judgment, as well as any promises.

"Let's make this quick," he said. "I've got to get Grandma to Purls Gone Wild."

Purls Gone Wild? I could totally see his grandmother fitting right in to a group like that.

Tomorrow I had two objectives: I had to get back to work, and I had to get Mandee out of jail. Basically, I needed to put all of this behind me, and that meant I had to get busy nailing down some answers.

I was getting close. I could feel it, like a wolf sensing prey hiding just out of sight.

CHAPTER 17

"So, where does this leave us?" Gabby asked once we were back in my car. "Any other suspects?"

I sighed, beginning to get a headache from the rush of adrenaline compounded with pulsating questions. The good news was that Reef was asleep in the back, so I had a moment to breathe and think.

I stared out the front window at the dark parking lot stretched before us and the fast food restaurant at the street. Thank goodness, I wasn't craving meat anymore like I had been when I was pregnant. Talk about feeling like a hypocrite.

"Provided that Brian's alibi really does hold up . . . I don't know," I finally said.

"Maybe we need to widen the circle of suspects. Sometimes the most unexpected person is connected and responsible. Is there anyone else you talked to? Maybe someone who seemed innocent or even helpful, but who could somehow be involved?"

I let my head fall back against the rest behind me

and stared out into the dark night. I racked my brain for another idea. So far every lead that had seemed promising had fizzled into nothing. "I suppose there was the neighbor across the hall from Tag. He was drinking before ten a.m., which indicates to me that he could have some problems."

"I grew up around that, so I concur with your conclusion," Gabby said. "Does this neighbor have motive, means, or opportunity?"

I shrugged. "Opportunity, I guess. He's probably seen people grab Patrick's spare key from beneath the doormat. That's all I know. There was also another neighbor in the building who was very adamant when telling the police about Mandee's argument with Tag over Zumba. Maybe she protested so much to take the attention off herself."

"It's a possibility."

Anything was at this point. My two main suspects apparently had alibis. I was no good at this solving mysteries thing. I should just stick with my crusades to help animals. However, I wasn't feeling that great about my work there either lately.

"Who am I kidding? All of this is a stretch. What if someone I haven't even looked at did this? Or what if the police are right? What if Mandee is somehow accidentally responsible for this? Or what if it was just a terrible mistake? Maybe I've been wasting all my time on nothing." I almost wanted to cry again, but I didn't allow myself.

"Don't give up. Not yet." She paused. "I'm curious, Sierra. Did Mandee ever tell you where she left that crowbar that was later found in the dumpster?"

I tried to recall our conversation. "She said she used it on the dishwasher. She's a bit of a slob, so I'd bet she left the crowbar on the kitchen counter afterward—wherever was most convenient. She said she didn't throw it away until the next day, after she had the brilliant realization as she slept. Why?"

"I know you're tired, but can we go back to Patrick's apartment one more time?" Gabby asked.

My need for closure superseded my need for rest at the moment. "Sure. Why?"

"There's just one thing I want to check out. It's a hunch."

Reef was currently sleeping, Chad was out of town, and I didn't have to be at work for twelve more hours. It sounded like a win-win to me.

"Why not?" I said.

I put the car in reverse and set off to find more answers.

***

"You're here again," the drunk neighbor from across the hall said when we walked into the building.

Could this man have anything to do with all this? I hadn't even begun to explore what his history with Tag or Patrick might be. I was simply taking the man's word for it that he and Tag used to be chummy.

At the same time, I was nearly too exhausted to start all over from scratch. I hoped Gabby's reasoning for wanting to come to Patrick's apartment had merit. Knowing Gabby, it did. She had an eye for things other people missed.

"Yes, we're back. Still trying to find some answers," I finally said to the neighbor.

"It's like Grand Central around here lately."

His words caused me to pause. "What do you mean? Exactly who else has been by?"

"This guy who looked like he could tear my head off with one hand tied behind his back stopped by about thirty minutes ago," he said. "The word 'Viking' was stitched into his jacket, and that seemed like a perfect description. He was looking for Patrick. I told him he was out of town."

My throat constricted. Members of that motorcycle gang were still looking for Patrick. Were they angry enough to kill him?

Maybe, just maybe, Gabby was right and I'd drawn a circle that wasn't large enough. However, the last thing I wanted was to start back at the beginning.

"I take it there have been other people also?" Gabby said. "Besides the Viking guy."

"Now you guys are here. That other chick was staying here before that. The police have been in and out. That's not to mention my mom. Suddenly, she's Mrs. Social and she's having knitting club at our place every week."

"Are you always here to see everything?" I asked, curious how he had so much time.

"I'm outta work on disability. Hurt my back working construction."

"I see."

I didn't offer any other information. I really just wanted to wrap up this conversation and go inside Patrick's place.

Finally, he took the hint, said goodnight, and disappeared into his apartment. As soon as he was gone, we hurried up the stairs. I grabbed the key from its hiding spot, and we scrambled inside Patrick's apartment. I made sure to lock the door behind us.

We needed to be careful, just in case those motorcycle guys came back.

"Okay, why are we here?" I finally asked.

"I want to look at that vent."

"The vent?" I repeated, trying to follow her reasoning.

"It's just a hunch. It could be nothing. But, at this point, what have we got to lose?"

We walked back to the snake room. I kept Reef close to me, just in case there were any more delinquent snakes around. Reef was not going out of my sight while I was in this apartment.

Gabby knelt down at the vent. She pulled the cover in and out, in and out, several times. Finally, she stood and stared down at it.

"I'm trying to follow," I told her. "I really am. But I have no idea what you're doing."

Her gaze remained on the vent. "Why did someone need to pry this from the floor?"

I shrugged. "Because it was in there too tight?"

She shook her head. "But it wasn't. Even though it's slightly dented now, it's not tight. Based on the hole in the floor and the size of the vent cover, it never was too tight."

"I'm still not following. I blame it on my lack of sleep lately. Why does it matter if it was tight or not?"

Her hand went to her hip and she started doing that pacing thing again. "Whoever used that crowbar didn't need to use it to pry the vent from a tight space. They could have easily used their fingertips. They used it for another reason."

"To implicate Mandee and show malicious intent?" I asked.

"That's a good guess. But there were other ways someone could have implicated her. Besides, how did they know she used the crowbar and that her prints would be there?"

"Good question."

She paused and nodded as if her thoughts were finally coming together. "I think they used it because they couldn't bend down to the floor to remove it."

"You mean . . . like someone with a bad back?" My thoughts went to the neighbor across the hall.

"Possibly."

I nodded as her theory sank in. "You're right. Someone probably looked around the apartment for something to help get that vent cover off. This person found the crowbar that Mandee had used on the dishwasher, borrowed it, and then put it in the trash on their way out, just in case any evidence had been left. They wanted to cover up evidence they'd used it, just to be on the safe side."

"Sounds plausible."

"This same person may have played with the latch on Chalice's enclosure to make it extra easy for the snake to get out also. Besides, Mandee did leave for a few hours that night, so someone had enough time. Knowing Mandee, she probably posted online that she was going to a *My Little Pony* marathon."

"Maybe those marks on the floor were from a snare pole—I think that's what they're called. Maybe that was the original plan but it didn't work out.

"Who has a pole?"

"Jim, but he has an alibi."

"Airtight?"

"I suppose. Unless the vet I talked to is lying. I wouldn't put it past Jim to pay him off."

"I have a feeling this person used gloves. That way he didn't leave any prints, and he covered his tracks."

"You're probably right. The question is who?"

"That, my friend, is going to take some more investigating."

CHAPTER 18

At 4:30 a.m., I woke up and I knew with clarity who the killer was.

And I also knew how to handle the fate of Chalice.

Now I had to figure out how to take what I knew and prove it beyond the shadow of reasonable doubt.

It was too early to deal with Tag's killer, so instead I spent the morning drafting emails to people who might be able to help me with the Chalice situation. As soon as I knew something for sure, I'd call the reporters who'd left me endless messages this weekend.

I sent those emails off, fed and dressed Reef, fed and dressed myself, and then called Gabby. I explained to her what was going on and talked my plan through.

What would I do without her?

She agreed to come over and keep Reef for a couple of hours. Just in case things went south, I didn't want my baby to be there. But I really hoped that things wouldn't go south.

I arrived at Bunch Systems before it opened. I

stayed in my sedan and stared at the building, waiting for the first sign of life. It appeared empty, so, as I waited, I formulated exactly what I was going to say.

Finally, the light popped on and I saw people moving inside.

Before putting my plan into action, I put in a call to Detective DePalma and asked him to meet me here. That meant I had about twenty minutes to make this work and to stay alive.

I really hoped this worked. Otherwise, I was going to be in trouble.

Grandma sat behind the front desk again, watching something on the computer and polishing her cane when I walked in. Her eyes lit with recognition when she saw me.

"You again," she muttered. "Why'd you come back?"

"I need to speak with Brian again."

She stared hard at me. "Why?"

I had to remain calm. "That's something I'd like to discuss with him."

"Maybe he doesn't want to discuss it with you." She stared me down with her best mafia glare.

"Why don't you let me ask him about that?"

Her lips twitched in a sneer. "Fine."

This time she didn't bother to get up and get him. She hollered down the hallway. "Brian, you have company. She looks like a mean one."

I wasn't sure whether I wanted to sneer myself or look amused.

Brian appeared from the back hallway a moment later, a little Yorkie following at his feet. When he spotted me, he nearly stopped in his tracks. His shoulders drooped, and he sighed. Apparently, I'd exhausted him during our conversation last night.

"Haven't we talked enough?" he said, slowing down considerably.

"Not quite yet."

He stopped in front of me, as bristly as ever. "Why are you here? I have nothing else to say."

I got right to the point, mentally calculating that I had thirteen minutes until the police arrived. "I know who sent that snake down the vent into Tag's apartment."

He blinked but otherwise remained motionless. "Who?"

I took a play from Gabby's book and began to pace. "Someone who wanted revenge on Tag after he posted that video of you online."

He had the nerve to actually roll his eyes. "I told you I considered that, but I didn't do anything."

Just then, Detective DePalma stepped inside. He didn't look happy, but at least he was here. And early, at that.

This was my big moment, where I had to give it everything I had to sell my theory.

"Mrs. Davis. Here I am. Now, what's the purpose of this?" he asked.

"You've arrested the wrong person in the death of Tag Wilson."

"The evidence tells a different story. The evidence says Mandee Melkins is guilty of negligence."

I continued to pace. "No, your interpretation of the evidence tells a different story. What really happened is this: Tag Wilson wasn't a nice man. In fact, he was bitter and desperate for money after losing his job. He was mad at Brian for firing him. In retaliation, he followed Brian one day. I can't tell you what his initial motivation was. Maybe to beg for his job back. Maybe to jump him."

Brian grunt-laughed, as if the idea was ridiculous.

"Continue," the detective said, narrowing his eyes. "And please speed this up."

"To Tag's surprise, he saw his former boss go to a comic convention dressed as a superhero. He caught it all on video. He threatened that if Brian didn't give him back his job, he'd post it online."

"Is that true?" the detective asked, his gaze flicking to Brian.

Brian nodded, his face red with embarrassment. "It is."

"Of course, Brian knew he couldn't allow himself to be blackmailed. He hoped that Tag was just talking trash. But he wasn't. He posted the video. It got thousands of views. People on online forums started mocking Brian. Some even left comments in their reviews of his company. It was bad for business, to say the least. It was also humiliating."

"This is all very interesting, but what's this have to do with the snake?" Detective DePalma asked.

"I'm getting to the pearl. I promise. Brian openly talked in the office about using Chalice to scare Tag. Everyone knew Tag was afraid of snakes. It would be the perfect setup. Brian never wanted anyone to get hurt. He just wanted to embarrass Tag. However, he changed his mind before he could put his plan into action."

"Then why am I here?" The detective narrowed his eyes even more.

"Someone else overheard Brian's plan and thought it was a good idea. They also knew how humiliated Brian was and thought Tag was evil as a result. This person snuck into Patrick's apartment. It's not hard to get into because there's a key under the front doormat. When they got inside, this person realized that the vent was on the floor and not in the wall, like it is in some apartments. Due to some physical ailments, this person couldn't reach the floor and needed a back-up plan. They grabbed the crowbar and used it to pull the vent from the floor. If you check it, you'll find that the vent never fit tightly into the cutout in the floor."

The detective nodded, curiosity creeping into his gaze. I had his attention now. "Continue. Why couldn't this person reach the vent?"

"Bad back, to say the least."

The detective glanced at Brian. "You have a bad back?"

Brian shook his head, his arms crossed over his chest. "No."

"It wasn't Brian," I told him. "The truth eluded me

for a while. But then I found these marks on the floor in Patrick's apartment. They were about the size of a nickel, and I saw them every foot or so."

"What was it?"

I glanced at Grandma. "It was a cane."

"You're blaming my grandma?" Brian asked. "Lady, you're crazy."

"Ask her," I said.

"That's ridiculous."

"We can clear this up right here with one little question," I continued.

"Go ahead, ma'am," Detective DePalma said. "Answer the question. Were you in that apartment?"

Grandma was silent a moment before trying to stand. "I can't have no one picking on my boy."

"Grandma!" Brian nearly fell over. "I'm a grown man. What were you thinking? Tell me this isn't true."

"Tag needed to be taught a lesson. I never meant for him to die. Who would have thought that he'd been out working at a farm that day and smell like livestock? What lousy timing."

Brian ran a hand through his hair. "Grandma . . . you shouldn't have. I was ready to let this go."

"Yeah? Well, I wasn't. No one messes with a Bunch. No one." She waved her cane. "That video was posted all over the Internet, and he needed to learn his lesson."

"So you're admitting to tampering with the vent?" the detective said.

She scowled again and nodded. "I may have

messed with the latches on top of the tank also. I figured it was just a matter of time until someone figured it out. I couldn't reach that confounded vent cover for the life of me."

"Don't say another word without a lawyer, Grandma," Brian said. "You've already said way too much."

"How did you figure out how to get into Patrick's apartment?" I asked.

"Easy. I became friends with the woman who lives across the hall from Tag and her good-for-nothing son. I didn't do it on purpose, but I met her once when Tag had us over to eat. We became friends and she even invited me to be a part of her knitting group—Purls Gone Wild. She told me that Patrick hid his key under the doormat. It wasn't a secret."

"But if you couldn't reach the vent, how could you reach the key?" I asked.

She raised her cane. "I have a magnet on the bottom of this. It snagged the keyring. I call this my all-in-one cane. Multi-purpose. It's the latest craze."

That also explained the marks on the floor.

The detective shook his head. "I'm going to have to take you down to the station, ma'am."

She stood, even though it took her nearly five minutes to do so. "Fine. I've lived in the Bronx. I can handle your jail."

"Detective?" I said.

He turned toward me. "Yes?"

"Mandee is supposed to go before the judge soon."
He scowled. "I'll put in a phone call."

CHAPTER 19

By the end of the following week, life had started feeling halfway normal again. I was home from work, I'd left a dinner of vegetable soup in the crockpot for myself, and Reef seemed content in his bouncy seat. He'd actually let me sleep six hours straight for the past two nights.

Gabby called me from Mythical Falls, where she and the rest of the gang were working, and I gave her the rundown of what had happened since Monday morning. I hadn't been able to go as planned because Reef came down with an ear infection. It was probably just as well since I was busy helping Mandee sort through the fiasco, run damage control at Animal Protective Services, and try to better organize my time so I didn't feel so frantic.

Basically, this was what had happened since last week: Authorities were holding Grandma Bunch for the death of Tag Wilson. The tough, old broad seemed determined to do well for herself, and I was sure she'd keep the other ladies in jail straight until she got her fair and speedy trial.

The night after she was arrested, three members of the Vikings were also arrested. Apparently, they'd found Patrick and cornered him. To get out of the situation, Patrick had told them how much Chalice was worth. As a result, members of the Vikings had tried to break into Animal Control and steal the snake. Thankfully, they were all behind bars now.

And, finally, there was Chalice. I'd contacted an animal rescue group down in Florida that specialized in reptiles. They were closely affiliated with a well-known zoo, and they'd agreed to take the snake.

They were trained experts who knew how to handle animals like Chalice, so the snake would get a fair shot. I didn't approve of what the snake had done—not by any means. But the animal hadn't been aggressive. I felt that under the right circumstances, Chalice could thrive.

Animal Control had agreed, probably happy to have the public relations nightmare off their hands. Chalice would be taking a trip south by the end of the week.

Mandee was released, and now I was counting down the days until her internship with me ended. I'd actually relegated her to work under Chloe, which made my strong-willed employee feel special.

Patrick had returned to his apartment. He still had a huge debt to pay off, but, thanks to the sale of some of his photographs, he should be able to do just that. In fact, he'd even given me one, which I'd hung in my living room.

"It sounds like a job well done, Detective Davis," Gabby said when we talked on the phone. "I've trained you well, my little Padawan."

"Ha ha. I did, for a moment, feel like you." I picked up Reef and stared at his handsome little face. I was so glad he was feeling better. His ear infection had meant hours and hours of fussing.

"Feels good to solve a case, doesn't it?"

I raised my eyebrows. "It feels good to have that off my plate."

"Maybe you should take some time off."

I shrugged, even though she couldn't see me. "I don't know yet. I just feel so rattled lately as I've been trying to balance everything. I want Reef to have a better childhood than I did. I know that means I can't work eighty hours a week and relegate his care to babysitters. It's just not what I want for his future."

"I get that. Our pasts shape our futures."

"I just don't know if we can live without my income right now, though."

"I was actually hoping that you might come to Mythical Falls . . . tomorrow."

"Tomorrow? Aren't you guys getting ready to leave?"

"We will be leaving soon, but I was hoping you could do me a favor."

"Sure thing. Like what?"

"Like, go into my closet and find a certain dress that I left there."

I nearly snorted. "I didn't think you owned any dresses."

"Well, I do own one. It's white and long. It has a veil."

I gasped. "What? Your wedding dress?"

She chuckled. "Yes, my wedding dress. It's a long story, but I'd love to tell you about it in person."

"I'd love to hear it in person."

"So what do you say?"

I didn't have to think about it anymore. "I'll be there."

"I told you from the start that it would be fun to hang out. And what better place to do that than a creepy, old theme park?"

"I couldn't have said it better."

We both chuckled.

As we hung up, I looked at Reef again. "Just one more adventure, okay? Then no more adventures for a while, okay?"

He cooed back at me.

Somehow, I knew there were going to be plenty of adventures in our future. Even after West Virginia.

And I was okay with that.

###

RATTLED

If you enjoyed *Rattled*, stayed tuned for *Caged*:

CHRISTY
BARRITT
AWARD-WINNING AUTHOR

CAGED

It's the most exotic case
Sierra's ever encountered.

THE
SIERRA FILES
BOOK 4

If you enjoyed this book, you may also enjoy:

Squeaky Clean Mysteries

Hazardous Duty (Book 1)

On her way to completing a degree in forensic science, Gabby St. Claire drops out of school and starts her own crime-scene cleaning business. When a routine cleaning job uncovers a murder weapon the police overlooked, she realizes that the wrong person is in jail. But the owner of the weapon is a powerful foe . . . and willing to do anything to keep Gabby quiet. With the help of her new neighbor, Riley Thomas, a man whose life and faith fascinate her, Gabby seeks to find the killer before another murder occurs.

Suspicious Minds (Book 2)

In this smart and suspenseful sequel to *Hazardous Duty*, crime-scene cleaner Gabby St. Claire finds herself stuck doing mold remediation to pay the bills. Her first day on the job, she uncovers a surprise in the crawlspace of a dilapidated home: Elvis, dead as a doornail and still wearing his blue-suede shoes. How could she possibly keep her nose out of a case like this?

It Came Upon a Midnight Crime (Book 2.5, a Novella)

Someone is intent on destroying the true meaning of Christmas—at least, destroying anything that hints of it. All around crime-scene cleaner Gabby St. Claire's hometown, anything pointing to Jesus as "the reason for the season" is being sabotaged. The crimes become more twisted as dismembered body parts are found at the vandalisms. Someone is determined to destroy Christmas . . . but Gabby is just as determined to find the Grinch and let peace on earth and goodwill prevail.

Organized Grime (Book 3)

Gabby St. Claire knows her best friend, Sierra, isn't guilty of killing three people in what appears to be an eco-terrorist attack. But Sierra has disappeared, her only contact a frantic phone call to Gabby proclaiming she's being hunted. Gabby is determined to prove her friend is innocent and to keep Sierra alive. While trying to track down the real perpetrator, Gabby notices a disturbing trend at the crime scenes she's cleaning, one that ties random crimes together—and points to Sierra as the guilty party. Just what has her friend gotten herself involved in?

Dirty Deeds (Book 4)

"Promise me one thing. No snooping. Just for one week." Gabby St. Claire knows that her fiancé's request is a simple one she should be able to honor. After all, Riley's law school reunion and attorneys' conference at a posh resort is a chance for them to get away from the mysteries Gabby often finds herself involved in as a crime-scene cleaner. Then an old friend of Riley's goes missing. Gabby suspects one of Riley's buddies might be behind the disappearance. When the missing woman's mom asks Gabby for help, how can she say no?

The Scum of All Fears (Book 5)

Gabby St. Claire is back to crime-scene cleaning and needs help after a weekend killing spree fills her work docket. A serial killer her fiancé put behind bars has escaped. His last words to Riley were: *I'll get out, and I'll get even.* Pictures of Gabby are found in the man's prison cell, messages are left for Gabby at crime scenes, someone keeps slipping in and out of her apartment, and her temporary assistant disappears. The search for answers becomes darker when Gabby realizes she's dealing with a criminal who is truly the scum of the earth. He will do anything to make Gabby's and Riley's lives a living nightmare.

To Love, Honor, and Perish (Book 6)

Just when Gabby St. Claire's life is on the right track, the unthinkable happens. Her fiancé, Riley Thomas, is shot and in life-threatening condition only a week before their wedding. Gabby is determined to figure out who pulled the trigger, even if investigating puts her own life at risk. As she digs deeper into the case, she discovers secrets better left alone. Doubts arise in her mind, and the one man with answers lies on death's doorstep. Then an old foe returns and tests everything Gabby is made of—physically, mentally, and spiritually. Will all she's worked for be destroyed?

Mucky Streak (Book 7)

Gabby St. Claire feels her life is smeared with the stain of tragedy. She takes a short-term gig as a private investigator—a cold case that's eluded detectives for ten years. The mass murder of a wealthy family seems impossible to solve, but Gabby brings more clues to light. Add to the mix a flirtatious client, travels to an exciting new city, and some quirky—albeit temporary—new sidekicks, and things get complicated. With every new development, Gabby prays that her "mucky streak" will end and the future will become clear. Yet every answer she uncovers leads her closer to danger—both for her life and for her heart.

Foul Play (Book 8)

Gabby St. Claire is crying "foul play" in every sense of the phrase. When the crime-scene cleaner agrees to go undercover at a local community theater, she discovers more than backstage bickering, atrocious acting, and rotten writing. The female lead is dead, and an old classmate who has staked everything on the musical production's success is about to go under. In her dual role of investigator and star of the show, Gabby finds the stakes rising faster than the opening-night curtain. She must face her past and make monumental decisions, not just about the play but also concerning her future relationships and career. Will Gabby find the killer before the curtain goes down—not only on the play, but also on life as she knows it?

Broom and Gloom (Book 9)

Gabby St. Claire is determined to get back in the saddle again. While in Oklahoma for a forensic conference, she meets her soon-to-be stepbrother, Trace Ryan, an up-and-coming country singer. A woman he was dating has disappeared, and he suspects a crazy fan may be behind it. Gabby agrees to investigate, as she tries to juggle her conference, navigate being alone in a new place, and locate a woman who may not want to be found. She discovers that sometimes taking life by the horns means staring danger in the face, no matter the consequences.

Dust and Obey (Book 10)

When Gabby St. Claire's ex-fiancé, Riley Thomas, asks for her help in investigating a possible murder at a couples retreat, she knows she should say no. She knows she should run far, far away from the danger of both being around Riley and the crime. But her nosy instincts and determination take precedence over her logic. Gabby and Riley must work together to find the killer. In the process, they have to confront demons from their past and deal with their present relationship.

Thrill Squeaker (Book 11)

An abandoned theme park. An unsolved murder. A decision that will change Gabby's life forever. Restoring an old amusement park and turning it into a destination resort seems like a fun idea for former crime-scene cleaner Gabby St. Claire. The side job gives her the chance to spend time with her friends, something she's missed since beginning a new career. The job turns out to be more than Gabby bargained for when she finds a dead body on her first day. Add to the mix legends of Bigfoot, creepy clowns, and ghostlike remnants of happier times at the park, and her stay begins to feel like a rollercoaster ride. Someone doesn't want the decrepit Mythical Falls to open again, but just how far is this person willing to go to ensure this venture fails? As the stakes rise and danger creeps closer, will Gabby be able to restore things in her own life that time has destroyed—including broken relationships? Or is her future closer to the fate of the doomed Mythical Falls?

Cunning Attractions (Book 12)

Coming soon

While You Were Sweeping, a Riley Thomas Novella

Riley Thomas is trying to come to terms with life after a traumatic brain injury turned his world upside down. Away from everything familiar—including his crime-scene-cleaning former fiancée and his career as a social-rights attorney—he's determined to prove himself and regain his old life. But when he claims he witnessed his neighbor shoot and kill someone, everyone thinks he's crazy. When all evidence of the crime disappears, even Riley has to wonder if he's losing his mind.

Note: *While You Were Sweeping* is a spin-off mystery written in conjunction with the Squeaky Clean series featuring crime-scene cleaner Gabby St. Claire.

The Sierra Files

Pounced (Book 1)

Animal-rights activist Sierra Nakamura never expected to stumble upon the dead body of a coworker while filming a project nor get involved in the investigation. But when someone threatens to kill her cats unless she hands over the "information," she becomes more bristly than an angry feline. Making matters worse is the fact that her cats—and the investigation—are driving a wedge between her and her boyfriend, Chad. With every answer she uncovers, old hurts rise to the surface and test her beliefs. Saving her cats might mean ruining everything else in her life. In the fight for survival, one thing is certain: either pounce or be pounced.

Hunted (Book 2)

Who knew a stray dog could cause so much trouble? Newlywed animal-rights activist Sierra Nakamura Davis must face her worst nightmare: breaking the news she eloped with Chad to her ultra-opinionated tiger mom. Her perfectionist parents have planned a vow-renewal ceremony at Sierra's lush childhood home, but a neighborhood dog ruins the rehearsal dinner when it shows up toting what appears to be a fresh human bone.

While dealing with the dog, a nosy neighbor, and an old flame turning up at the wrong times, Sierra hunts for answers. Her journey of discovery leads to more than just who committed the crime.

Pranced (Book 2.5, a Christmas novella)

Sierra Nakamura Davis thinks spending Christmas with her husband's relatives will be a real Yuletide treat. But when the animal-rights activist learns his family has a reindeer farm, she begins to feel more like the Grinch. Even worse, when Sierra arrives, she discovers the reindeer are missing. Sierra fears the animals might be suffering a worse fate than being used for entertainment purposes. Can Sierra set aside her dogmatic opinions to help get the reindeer home in time for the holidays? Or will secrets tear the family apart and ruin Sierra's dream of the perfect Christmas?

Holly Anna Paladin Mysteries

Random Acts of Murder (Book 1)

When Holly Anna Paladin is given a year to live, she embraces her final days doing what she loves most—random acts of kindness. But one of her extreme good deeds goes horribly wrong, implicating her in a string of murders. Holly is suddenly thrust into a different kind of fight for her life. Could it also be random that the detective assigned to the case is her old high school crush and present-day nemesis? Will Holly find the killer before he ruins what is left of her life? Or will she spend her final days alone and behind bars?

Random Acts of Deceit (Book 2)

"Break up with Chase Dexter, or I'll kill him." Holly Anna Paladin never expected such a gut-wrenching ultimatum. With home invasions, hidden cameras, and bomb threats, Holly must make some serious choices. Whatever she decides, the consequences will either break her heart or break her soul. She tries to match wits with the Shadow Man, but the more she fights, the deeper she's drawn into the perilous situation. With her sister's wedding problems and the riots in the city, Holly has nearly reached her breaking point. She must stop this mystery man before someone she loves dies. But the deceit is threatening to pull her under . . . six feet under.

Random Acts of Murder (Book 3)

When Holly Anna Paladin's boyfriend, police detective Chase Dexter, says he's leaving for two weeks and can't give any details, she wants to trust him. But when she discovers Chase may be involved in some unwise and dangerous pursuits, she's compelled to intervene. Holly gets a run for her money as she's swept into the world of horseracing. The stakes turn deadly when a dead body surfaces and suspicion is cast on Chase. At every turn, more trouble emerges, making Holly question what she holds true about her relationship and her future. Just when she thinks she's on the homestretch, a dark horse arises. Holly might lose everything in a nail-biting fight to the finish.

Random Acts of Scrooge (Book 3.5)

Christmas is supposed to be the most wonderful time of the year, but a real-life Scrooge is threatening to ruin the season's good will. Holly Anna Paladin can't wait to celebrate Christmas with family and friends. She loves everything about the season—celebrating the birth of Jesus, singing carols, and baking Christmas treats, just to name a few. But when a local family needs help, how can she say no? Holly's community has come together to help raise funds to save the home of Greg and Babette Sullivan, but a Bah-Humburgler has snatched the canisters of cash. Holly and her boyfriend, police detective Chase Dexter, team up to catch the Christmas crook. Will they succeed in collecting enough cash to cover the Sullivans' overdue bills? Or will someone succeed in ruining Christmas for all those involved?

Random Acts of Guilt **(Book 4)**

Coming soon

Carolina Moon Series

Home Before Dark (Book 1)

Nothing good ever happens after dark. Country singer Daleigh McDermott's father often repeated those words. Now, her father is dead. As she's about to flee back to Nashville, she finds his hidden journal with hints that his death was no accident. Mechanic Ryan Shields is the only one who seems to believe Daleigh. Her father trusted the man, but her attraction to Ryan scares her. She knows her life and career are back in Nashville and her time in the sleepy North Carolina town is only temporary. As Daleigh and Ryan work to unravel the mystery, it becomes obvious that someone wants them dead. They must rely on each other—and on God—if they hope to make it home before the darkness swallows them.

Gone By Dark (Book 2)

Charity White can't forget what happened ten years earlier when she and her best friend, Chloe, cut through the woods on their way home from school. A man abducted Chloe, who hasn't been seen since. Charity has tried to outrun the memories and guilt. What if they hadn't taken that shortcut? Why wasn't Charity kidnapped instead of Chloe? And why weren't the police able to track down the bad guy? When Charity receives a mysterious letter that promises answers, she returns to North Carolina in search of closure and the peace that has eluded her. With the help of her new neighbor, Police Officer Joshua Haven, Charity begins to track down mysterious clues. They soon discover that they must work together or both of them will be swallowed by the looming darkness.

Cape Thomas Mysteries:

Dubiosity (Book 1)

Savannah Harris vowed to leave behind her old life as an investigative reporter. But when two migrant workers go missing, her curiosity spikes. As more eerie incidents begin afflicting the area, each works to draw Savannah out of her seclusion and raise the stakes—for her and the surrounding community. Even as Savannah's new boarder, Clive Miller, makes her feel things she thought long forgotten, she suspects he's hiding something too, and he's not the only one. As secrets emerge and danger closes in, Savannah must choose between faith and uncertainty. One wrong decision might spell the end . . . not just for her but for everyone around her. Will she unravel the mystery in time, or will doubt get the best of her?

Disillusioned (Book 2)

Coming soon

Standalones:

The Good Girl

Tara Lancaster can sing "Amazing Grace" in three harmonies, two languages, and interpret it for the hearing impaired. She can list the Bible canon backward, forward, and alphabetized. The only time she ever missed church was when she had pneumonia and her mom made her stay home. Then her life shatters and her reputation is left in ruins. She flees halfway across the country to dog-sit, but the quiet anonymity she needs isn't waiting at her sister's house. Instead, she finds a knife with a threatening message, a fame-hungry friend, a too-hunky neighbor, and evidence of . . . a ghost? Following all the rules has gotten her nowhere. And nothing she learned in Sunday School can tell her where to go from there.

Death of the Couch Potato's Wife (Suburban Sleuth Mysteries)

You haven't seen desperate until you've met Laura Berry, a career-oriented city slicker turned suburbanite housewife. Well-trained in the big-city commandment, "mind your own business," Laura is persuaded by her spunky seventy-year-old neighbor, Babe, to check on another neighbor who hasn't been seen in days. She finds Candace Flynn, wife of the infamous "Couch King," dead, and at last has a reason to get up in the morning. Someone is determined to stop her from digging deeper into the death of her neighbor, but Laura is just as determined to figure out who is behind the death-by-poisoned-pork-rinds.

Imperfect

Since the death of her fiancé two years ago, novelist Morgan Blake's life has been in a holding pattern. She has a major case of writer's block, and a book signing in the mountain town of Perfect sounds as perfect as its name. Her trip takes a wrong turn when she's involved in a hit-and-run: She hit a man, and he ran from the scene. Before fleeing, he mouthed the word "Help." First she must find him. In Perfect, she finds a small town that offers all she ever wanted. But is something sinister going on behind its cheery exterior? Was she invited as a guest of honor simply to do a book signing? Or was she lured to town for another purpose—a deadly purpose?

The Gabby St. Claire Diaries (a tween mystery series)

The Curtain Call Caper (Book 1)

Is a ghost haunting the Oceanside Middle School auditorium? What else could explain the disasters surrounding the play—everything from missing scripts to a falling spotlight and damaged props? Seventh-grader Gabby St. Claire has dreamed about being part of her school's musical, but a series of unfortunate events threatens to shut down the production. While trying to uncover the culprit and save her fifteen minutes of fame, she also has to manage impossible teachers, cliques, her dysfunctional family, and a secret she can't tell even her best friend. Will Gabby figure out who or what is sabotaging the show . . . or will it be curtains for her and the rest of the cast?

The Disappearing Dog Dilemma (Book 2)

Why are dogs disappearing around town? When two friends ask seventh-grader Gabby St. Claire for her help in finding their missing canines, Gabby decides to unleash her sleuthing skills to sniff out whoever is behind the act. But time management and relationships get tricky as worrisome weather, a part-time job, and a new crush interfere with Gabby's investigation. Will her determination crack the case? Or will shadowy villains, a penchant for overcommitting, and even her own heart put her in the doghouse?

The Bungled Bike Burglaries (Book 3)

Stolen bikes and a long-forgotten time capsule leave one amateur sleuth baffled and busy. Seventh-grader Gabby St. Claire is determined to bring a bike burglar to justice— and not just because mean girl Donabell Bullock is strong-arming her. But each new clue brings its own set of trouble. As if that's not enough, Gabby finds evidence of a decades-old murder within the contents of the time capsule, but no one seems to take her seriously. As her investigation heats up, will Gabby's knack for being in the wrong place at the wrong time with the wrong people crack the case? Or will it prove hazardous to her health?

Complete Book List

Squeaky Clean Mysteries:
#1 Hazardous Duty
#2 Suspicious Minds
#2.5 It Came Upon a Midnight Crime
#3 Organized Grime
#4 Dirty Deeds
#5 The Scum of All Fears
#6 To Love, Honor, and Perish
#7 Mucky Streak
#8 Foul Play
#9 Broom and Gloom
#10 Dust and Obey
#11 Thrill Squeaker
#12 Cunning Attractions (coming soon)

Squeaky Clean Companion Novella:
While You Were Sweeping

The Sierra Files:
#1 Pounced
#2 Hunted
#2.5 Pranced (a Christmas novella)
#3 Rattled

The Gabby St. Claire Diaries (a Tween Mystery series):
#1 The Curtain Call Caper
#2 The Disappearing Dog Dilemma

#3 The Bungled Bike Burglaries
Holly Anna Paladin Mysteries:
#1 Random Acts of Murder
#2 Random Acts of Deceit
#3 Random Acts of Malice
#3.5 Random Acts of Scrooge
#4 Random Acts of Guilt (coming soon)

Carolina Moon Series:
Home Before Dark
Gone By Dark
Wait Until Dark (coming soon)

Suburban Sleuth Mysteries:
#1 Death of the Couch Potato's Wife

Stand-alone Romantic-Suspense:
Keeping Guard
The Last Target
Race Against Time
Ricochet
Key Witness
Lifeline
High-Stakes Holiday Reunion
Desperate Measures
Hidden Agenda
Mountain Hideaway
Dark Harbor (coming soon)

<u>Cape Thomas Mysteries</u>
Dubiosity
Disillusioned (coming soon)

Standalone Romantic Mystery:
The Good Girl

Suspense:
Imperfect

Nonfiction:
Changed: True Stories of Finding God through Christian Music
The Novel in Me: The Beginner's Guide to Writing and Publishing a Novel

About the Author:

USA Today has called Christy Barritt's books "scary, funny, passionate, and quirky."

Christy writes both mystery and romantic suspense novels that are clean with underlying messages of faith. Her books have won the Daphne du Maurier Award for Excellence in Suspense and Mystery, have been twice nominated for the Romantic Times Reviewers' Choice Award, and have finaled for both a Carol Award and Foreword Magazine's Book of the Year.

She is married to her Prince Charming, a man who thinks she's hilarious—but only when she's not trying to be. Christy is a self-proclaimed klutz, an avid music lover who's known for spontaneously bursting into song, and a road trip aficionado.

When she's not working or spending time with her family, she enjoys singing, playing the guitar, and exploring small, unsuspecting towns where people have no idea how accident-prone she is.

Find Christy online at:

www.christybarritt.com

www.facebook.com/christybarritt

www.twitter.com/cbarritt

Sign up for Christy's newsletter to get information on all of her latest releases here:

www.christybarritt.com/newsletter-sign-up/

If you enjoyed this book, please consider leaving a review.

RATTLED